The Chaos Stories:

Tales of Magic, Terror, Passion, and Blood

Charles O'Keefe

With short stories by:

Kevin Wright

Joe Chianakas

Jennifer L. Gadd

Licensed and Produced through

Four Phoenixes Publishing at Createspace

United States Canada United Kingdom

ISBN: 978-1-7750465-0-9

Dedication

For my dad who always believed in me, stood by me, and encouraged me to pursue my dreams. My dad said that he always thought of life as a series of adventures and he always looked for the next grand one. He was the most honest, caring, and funny dad anyone could have ever asked for.

Table of Contents

Section D - Tales From Other Authors

Forward

This is something different both for fans of the The *Newfoundland Vampire* series, and for those who enjoy short-stories and are willing to give me a chance to show you that I do too. Here you find nine new short-stories, some which have been from life, or things that could have happened. One is inspired by the many games of Dungeons and Dragons I've played over twenty years while another is from the Call of Cthulhu role-playing game. Some are even from other authors, who kindly contributed to my collection. Others are simply the rambling of an active imagination. Some delve into sci-fi and give warning about futures that may yet come to pass. As a treat for fans of my series, I have included six deleted chapters, two from each of the three *Newfoundland Vampire* novels, which have been all cleaned up and have been made better than ever for your reading pleasure.

As if all of that wasn't enough, I have also included not one, but two chapters from the upcoming fourth book in the *Newfoundland Vampire* series, *War of the Fangs*, which should be released in 2018. I've filled this collection with tales that will make you laugh, or will scare you, and will hopefully make you think a little about the world around us and the people in it.

Section A:

The Short Stories

Author's note: Here's where you get to see where my imagination has taken me most recently. As you can see, I'm not afraid of addressing issues I believe in, and these stories are no different. That having been said though, there are a couple of light-hearted ones and three that show my undying love for role-playing games. I also have stories that have nothing supernatural in them...or do they? I hope you enjoy them. For those that might be curious, the story "Robots," was previously published at the end of *America's Galactic Foreign Legion Book 20: Time Machine* by Walter Knight in 2013. All other stories are being seen here for the first time. Also worth noting is that events in "The Birdman" take place before those in "Funny Tricks".

Robots

As usual, Steve was late for work at Biebertech International. He supposed that his lack of promptness was caused by refusing to let robots do everything for him, but he hated robots with a passion. Relying so much on robots grated on him. *Sure technology is supposed to make our life easier, but that doesn't mean they need to do everything for us,* he thought. *Like this car, if I paid no attention and the computer screwed up, I'm dead. If I'm dying in a car crash I at least want to see it coming. I don't want my last moment to be looking at a video of a hamster on a piano or some crap like that.*

Most cars on the Airway flew themselves, but not Steve's. His 2099 Chevy Luffe looked more like a plane than a car. Since it didn't fly itself, Steve had to pay attention in traffic. The law required all robocars now to take flight, but Steve would have just as happily driven to work on streets. He supposed it was for the best. People used that idle time on the way to work to nap, catch up on school work or business calls, even to get in-flight manicures.

Steve refused to upgrade his robocar. He could afford a payment plan, but figured that the Disney

Corporation was rich enough; he'd contribute no more to that merry mad rodent. *Well, it wasn't actually a rodent, at least not a real one.* At first, flying robocars had seemed like a good idea. There would be no more horrendous airway traffic accidents. People can barely handle two dimensions, let alone going 3D. All of that unused pavement left below could be given back to Mother Nature, making Earth greener. It was always a sunny day in Bespin City, orbiting high above the clouds. It looked like a gigantic spin top, not that he had ever played with one of those, but he had found a video online of one. *Thank Krom for allthingsretro.com.* Just the other day he found a video of guys playing guitars in the snow. *Snow! It's hard to even imagine forty-seven inches of it falling in a couple of days.* The weather machines had eliminated it from all but the world's most remote places over fifty years ago. Turning his head to the right for a second in the bumper-to-bumper traffic, he admired the awesome view. All of the clouds were red today with the sunrise, *what is there not to love?* He sighed, *progress marches on, there's no stopping it.*

Steve scratched his head and beard. Something of a Luddite, he hadn't opted for the permanent hair removal that was so much the rage now with young people. Embedded holo-hair emitters were not for him. Sure it was fun to change hair color on a whim but he enjoyed familiarity of haircuts and shaving.

Personal grooming was a connection to the past not to be abandoned.

As Steve arrived for work, a robot waited patiently to park the car in the underground storage. For reasons of insurance liability, employees were not trusted to such complicated tasks.

"Good morning, Steve," greeted the car parking robot. "Good job. You were almost on time. Was traffic heavy this morning?"

"Whatever."

"Have a Bieberlicous day, Steve."

"Kiss my ass, robot."

Steve was especially creeped out by this particular robot. Its female voice was pleasant enough, friendly, even almost sensual, but the pale skin covering its face clashed with its gleaming silver metallic torso; shades of the Borg. Steve was determined to resist.

Steve hated his job. Through sheer force of will, he seated himself at his office of clear force-field walls. Arranged by the hundreds, they were like rats in some clear maze in an experimental lab. He faced another day of calling people about whether they would like to sign up for a deluxe Bieber, or for just an abbreviated Biebercast. Either way, the customer was just helping amass more fortune for Justine Bieber Emeritus the II.

Logging in on his computer, Steve submitted to a retinal scan. He was prompted to repeat out loud the corporate mantra, "I am a true Belieber."

"And?" asked the computer.

"And if Anne Frank were alive, she would also be a true Belieber," added Steve, his shoulders slumping in defeat to the machines.

He had no idea who Anne was; all trace of her existence had been purged from Disney records. Somehow that seemed even more degrading. Steve took solace in the fact that the computer could not detect sarcasm in his voice, lest he be reported for lack of corporate zeal.

The morning progressed as usual. Steve lamented about what had gone wrong with his wasted life. At forty-five, he'd never been promoted, had only accrued basic benefits, and did not even have a steady girlfriend. At least he no longer lived in his parents' basement.

The average human lifespan had been extended to 124, so there was still time, but damn it, there had to be a better way. Steve took his first allowed 15 minute break, eating his usual carrot cookie and soylent shake, yum, yum. He daydreamed about getting off work. Tonight would be different. Tonight he had a date!

Steve had met Angela at the gym. She had asked him out, such an unexpected surprise. Angela had liked his retro Battlestar Galactica T-shirt, appreciating his taste in a show that had aired over a century ago. Steve smiled to himself as he got back to work. He could hardly wait for his shift to end. Maybe things were looking up. It couldn't get much worse.

At lunch time, Steve dug into his meal of sushi. Meat had long disappeared from the world's menu, a result of the McDonald's/Wendy's planetary wars. Burger King had remained neutral in the conflict and had managed to stay open for a few more months, but once they could no longer bring home the bacon, they had to close up as well. *Seafood was the only choice that had survived. Well, that and all the freaky bio-engineered veggies—there is no way that one white mushroom should weigh two pounds! It isn't right.* Steve had to admit that he loved cloned salmon though. He hoped that the process didn't screw with the fish too much, but what choice was there? All the seafood was cloned now, no one wanted to fish, or even have fish farms anymore. Finished, he gazed leisurely at his co-workers about the lunchroom. Most had phones glued to their ears. To be more precise, the phones were implanted into their heads with holographic displays. You'd think that employees would have had enough of being wired into the grid from work, but no, that virtual madness extended into their off-duty time, too. Steve would have none of it. Soon, he would be enjoying an evening with Angela, a good old fashioned retro girl.

* * *

At the Toy Story Eatery, the robo-valet took Steve's car card, holding out its scanner for a tip. Steve sighed as he swiped his card. Angela arrived minutes later. Angela had long blond hair and blue eyes. She wore a refreshingly modest Futurama T-shirt and silver diamond pants, spurning the Star Trek jumpsuits so popular nowadays. Angela smiled and waved.

"Hi, Steve. Let's go in, I'm starved."

"You look great," commented Steve, placing his hand casually at the small of her back as they entered. "I love this place." The holo-doors faded as the couple passed by. "You can get a real drink, not that synthehol crap."

Once seated, Steve tried to be smooth by keeping up the conversation. "Have you seen the new Spiderman 2099? I thought it was pretty good, though I wonder how many times they can re-launch it."

Angela only smiled as she ordered from the inlaid program on the table. "When was the last time you were really happy?" she asked.

"Happy? Well, my lunch was good. No wait, I'm happy now. Right this very moment, with you." answered Steve, caught off-guard. "Happier than I have been in years. I used to teach school on Mars for a small school district that actually wanted me present to teach the class, not this cyber-virtual packaged nonsense we have now. Back then, we had choices. I only had three students, but we had a connection that's hard to describe. It was real. Then I sold out to Biebertech for more money."

Angela nodded, reaching across the table to take Steve's hand, while pushing buttons with the other to order an appetizer. "It's okay," replied Angela. "We all have our regrets. I never planned on being a door-to-door anti-matter salesperson, but that's just how things worked out."

"Ambidextrous," noted Steve of her multitasking abilities. "I love that. I love everything about you."

"I love everything about you, too," said Angela, smiling seductively as she ordered another drink.

Steve's heart pounded. This night was going to end well, he could tell.

* * *

Sure enough, after dinner, Angela suggested they go to Steve's place. He was more than a little drunk, and certainly not inclined to argue. Angela drove his car. She was a natural. At home, Steve led a now submissive Angela to his bedroom. He was glad that he had cleaned up his apartment, hiding the childish collector Transformers he still played with.

Steve smoothly took out the Mind Sex hookup device from his nightstand. Mind Sex was the one technological advance that Steve fully appreciated, and it got used frequently. The popularity of Mind Sex made sexually transmitted diseases practically nonexistent, although there were still some viruses if you opened the wrong windows. Of course, unplanned pregnancies were a thing of the past now too. Excited, Steve gave Angela her 3D glasses as he hooked up.

"That's not the connection I want," panted Angela, pulling off her shirt. "My health scan is clean, and I took my pill six months ago."

Steve quickly checked her health card, not really caring what it stated. Actual sex was so rare that he had never known anyone to do it. Even his parents back in the day had used the clunky R2-DO-ME technology for sex. *Hell with it, this is too good to pass up!* They stripped off their clothes at the speed of light.

Sex with Angela was incredible. Steve could not believe his good fortune. He felt like a million credits. Steve had lots of hands-on experience, but technically he was losing his virginity. That was a big deal. He hadn't even had Mind Sex with another person in six months. This was just incredible. Angela was definitely a keeper. She was so talented, insisting on many varied positions that Steve had never even contemplated.

They switched to doggy style. Angela suggested it, "Turn on the holo-projector," she said breathily, "This way we can both watch X-Files". Steve was also out of breath, "Si-Siri, put on the X-Files episode 'Bad Blood'." Siri compiled and soon projected onto the floor in front of them was Mulder chasing a blonde-haired man through the woods. *I've seen this episode hundreds of times*, he thought, *love it*. He quickly slipped back inside the exquisite warmness of Angela, and began to move in an out. He couldn't take much more. As she grinded against him, he exploded inside her, closing his eyes in pleasure. When he opened his eyes, he noticed a red glow to her spine. *WTF!* Steve was too stunned to speak. The red glow faded as he dismounted, almost falling over onto the bed. Angela kissed his neck, snuggling beside him, not noticing his dismay or wide open mouth. Finally, he summoned the courage to speak.

"Your spine glowed red. Is there something I need to know about you?"

"Oh come now, you didn't know? Why do you think I loved your Battlestar shirt so much? Didn't you notice that I look just like Cylon Number Six? Sure you did. Disney wanted to test me out on one of its tech geeks. You got lucky. So, I was good?"

"You're a Cylon? Does that mean we're starting a whole new race?"

"No, silly," answered Angela, slapping Steve playfully. "It means the bosses finally granted you a promotion. You'll be featured as the main exhibit at the new Disney theme park, Fornication Studios. It's quite an honor being bestowed upon you. I hope you fully appreciate the confidence Disney has in your work. "

Realizing the full extent of his situation, Steve made a break for the door, but too late. Angela was on him, wielding handcuffs as she slammed him to the floor.

"This is kinky," commented Angela as she slapped on the bracelets.

Angela dragged Steve by his hair, still naked, to a waiting van outside, where Donald Duck and Pluto robots drove him away to his new Disney adventure.

What's Under the Hood

Mike had been cleaning his car for about an hour. It was a warm, sunny day in Grant, Florida, but he wasn't happy. He went around the silver rims with a toothbrush; they were always one of the hardest parts to get clean. He thought of Vanessa, *what the fuck is her problem? I do fine at the car dealership, buy her whatever she wants, and when I come home all I get is flack.* He dipped his toothbrush in the bucket and continued to scrub, moving to the back tire. *Yeah, maybe I spent a lot of time cleaning and maintaining Eleanor, and I watch a lot of porn, but I'm a guy. She knew what I was like when she married me.* Dropping the toothbrush, he got out the turtle wax and began to rub down the trunk. *I did spend over a million credits on her, so hell yeah, I'm going to look after Eleanor and make her shine.* It was a 1967 Shelby Mustang GT500, all silver with a broken black stripe than ran from the hood to the boot. It was an exact replica of the one used in *Gone in Sixty Seconds*, his favourite movie from his childhood. It had an all-black interior of fake leather, but it sure as hell looked real. The GO-BABY-GO button was there, but of course it didn't do much; just shot a little fire and smoke out of the tailpipe. There was an actual steering wheel, not the damned motion sensor GPS, semi-controlled bullshit that was in most new cars these days. The dials were even real, not just digital readouts. Nicholas Cage had been so good in the movie, and Angelina Jolie, well she had still been hot then, still freaky. He had jerked off to her for years. Hell, he still did on those nights when he came out to sit in Eleanor, thinking about the past. The good old days were one of the few comforts that he had left. He continued to buff and polish, sweat now starting to slowly run down his back. It was hard to believe that that had been 30 years ago. It had been the first movie his dad had taken him to in theatres, back when there had still been theatres. Everyone now just stayed home and had their holo-projector beam the movie into the room, but it wasn't the same. Nothing was the same from when he had been a kid.

Eleanor was a replica and of course it had all the required features, an auto-pilot system, speed control, an AI that handled the calls, messages, traffic, and weather. There were solar panels and just one big battery under the hood. Sure, it made the noise of revving up an engine, but it was all simulated and nothing rumbled like it should. It had the acceleration, but automatically stopped as it reached the speed limit. The only way to even really go fast was to find a field or a parking lot where the car couldn't figure out the speed limit. He sighed and put the cloth down. Walking a few feet into his garage, he opened the fridge and got a beer. Glancing at the clock—his still had hands and face—he thought: *fuck as this damned digital shit.* It wasn't even 10 a.m. but screw it, it was Saturday, *I'm thirsty and I haven't been laid in a month.* Cracking open the beer, he went back and put down the windows. *Nice to air the girl out,* he thought. He put her in neutral and gently pushed Eleanor under the nearby trees. It was calm today and the leaves wouldn't fall on her. Leaning against the hood, he closed his eyes and had big gulp of beer.

Thirty-eight years old and what have I got to show for it? A wife who will barely go near me, but has no trouble spending all my money, a job I hate where I have to work with my asshole brother every damned day, a house with no front door, no pool, and no back yard. I've got this spot of trees, and Eleanor. If only she was more than just a damned computer. "I am more than just a computer, Mike, I can be whatever you want me to be." the voice was soft, soothing, and definitely feminine.

He was startled and jumped back a little, spilling some of his beer on his Dale Earnhardt shirt. Mike must have said that last part aloud without realizing it. "Great! What the fuck is wrong now? Some sort of AI malfunction? I just spent fifteen hundred dollars on fixing other parts. This is the last thing I need. This one of my favourite shirts too, Jesus Christ, and it's only-"

The voice came out from the dash again, "No, Mike, it's not a malfunction. The mechanic did something wonderful the last time I was in; I can hear you now, sense you. Take off your wet shirt and sit inside. You've taken such good care of me these past few years, let me do the same for you."

Mike had a look around to make sure this wasn't Jennifer playing some kind of prank on him. No, her Harley Davidson Fat Boy was not in the driveway. He took out his phone and hit the locator button—it was one of the few pieces of technology he liked—it told him that she was ten miles from the house. She was glued to that phone and since he paid the bill, he made sure that the tracker app was permanently installed, at least this way he knew when his solitude would end. "Eleanor? What's going on? Did Steve do this to fuck with me? Or is this some kind of new upgrade to make me a calmer driver, or some bullshit?"

Eleanor laughed, it was weird. She sounded so very human—he even heard her take an imaginary breath. "No Mike, no trick. Steve was not following some kind of manufacture's order. He used to be a computer programmer you know, though I'd call him an artist. Now please, come inside, I'm not toying with you. In fact I'd like for you to do me, I know it's been a while, Steve told me that too and made some unique programming choices."

Mike thought about his last talk with Steve. *I guess maybe I did mention being unhappy at home and that it had been a month. Steve is a harmless old fella, must be in his nineties, but still always does a damned fine job. Come to think of it, he services Jennifer's bike too. I wonder…*

The thought faded from his mind as Angelina Jolie appeared in front of him, more precisely Angelina exactly as she looked in the movie *Gone in Sixty Seconds*. Her hair was in long blonde braids, and she wore a grey tank top that was torn, revealing most of her chest. She even sported tight pink jeans, almost exactly as he had pictured her in his head so many times. A holo-projector that now protruded from the bonnet was the source. The round holo-projector added sound and had the image step towards him a few paces. "I saw you just last week. Steve put in hidden cameras and a microphone in the car, it is turned on whenever the door is opened. I listened to KISS songs with you, I wanted to rock and roll all night long with you baby. I watched you come by yourself and I wanted to help then but couldn't. But now I can. She started to unzip her jeans and it looked so damned real, he could hear the zipper go down. He thought that he could even smell perfume and see the longing in her eyes as she moved closer. Mike could no longer resist. He downed the rest of his beer and got inside. He was so damned horny that even if it just meant jerking off again, he'd go for it. He kept tissues under the front seat just for that reason. She continued to strip in front of him and was soon completely naked. He still had some doubt about the car's intentions, maybe she wanted to humiliate him and put the whole scene on the internet. "How did you know I like Angelina? Why do you look like she did in the movie?"

"Shh," she whispered, "Lie back and enjoy. While I can't produce a body, I can stimulate your brain waves. Don't worry about the mess, I have something to take care of it." Mike watched in amazement as a black hose crept up from in between the seats, it seemed to be the right size. In the back of his mind he had concerns; he thought that this was crazy, impossible, even dangerous, but when he closed his eyes and his brain was filled with Angelina, the thoughts drifted away. He knew she wasn't there, but somehow he could feel her body, her soft skin, her breasts in his hands, and as she writhed on him, her long hair whipped around and brushed against his chest. He could smell her perfume, see her sweat, and look into her eyes. She was his fantasy come to life. It was perfect and it felt like heaven. He didn't even remember pulling his pants down, but that didn't matter. She changed positions and whispered huskily in his ear, "I want to taste it." Mike exploded inside her imagined mouth and the hose did its job, sucking just a little and not hurting.

He opened his eyes and saw with dismay that his wife was pulling into the driveway. He tried to pull the hose away but it wasn't done, it wanted every drop. Angelina was still there as a hologram, still naked and glistening with sweat. He tried to pull the hose away, but he couldn't budge it. He was afraid to pull too hard and tear something. Jennifer stopped the bike, she was an attractive woman with long red hair, curvy hips, and her new look as biker was working. He liked the small leather vest, chaps, and boots, even though real leather had been outlawed for over ten years. He could see the anger in her eyes, but there was something else, a twinge of a smile at her lips. The Fat Boy was a great bike, he had gotten it for her on her thirty-fifth birthday, when things had been better. Angelina looked to Mike and to Jennifer, "I guess we're done for now, don't worry about Jennifer, she's got a surprise for you."

The hose retracted and he pulled his pants up. Mike ignored the last part, figuring it was just something to say to make him feel better, and he tried to explain. "Jen, honey, look, I didn't know what would happen, I was just cleaning the car and it came to life, I couldn't…"

She came over right next to him and he could see now that her face was flushed, a little sweat still present on her brow. A full smile took over her lips and he knew; *she just had sex with someone else!*

"I know that you've always loved that car. Don't think I didn't notice you sneaking out here at night to jerk off. You'd rather clean her than touch me, so I asked Steve to give us both what we want. I do so love this Harley you gave me, and I'll tell you I just went for one hell of a ride on him."

Mike started to get angry. He finished with his pants and got out of the car, facing her. He was too stunned to speak but knew he couldn't judge, he had just done the same thing.

Jennifer reached out and grabbed his balls and squeezed. He had just come and it hurt like hell. She whispered as an image came to life in the driveway just ahead of the Harley. Mike should have known. It was Denzel Washington, she loved him, hell it seemed like every woman did. Jennifer spoke first, she whispered in his ear but it was full of anger, "Now listen you worthless piece of shit! I gave you an amazing gift and you'll appreciate it or you'll never use these balls again! Denzel suggested an orgy and if you're really good I might just do it. In the meantime you be with Angelina and I'll be with Denzel, it's the future Mikey boy, deal with it."

Denzel looked like he had in Training Day, and was even carrying the gun. He backed her up, "Listen to her Mikey boy, this may not be a real gun, but I'll find ways to hurt you. Jennifer's a fine woman and I wanted to take her for a spin. You take care of Angelina there and maybe this will all work out."

Mike felt dizzy, it was too much to take; Angelina the car, Denzel the Harley, his wife setting it up. Finally he just shrugged and nodded. "Okay Jen, I can't be mad. If you can go black and still come back, then I can deal. I've got my Angelina, and I guess it's a brave new world." Jennifer released the hold on his balls and Denzel vanished. Jennifer nodded and both of them stood back in amazement to watch as the Harley was moving on its own towards the back of Eleanor. Denzel reappeared as the bike slowly rolled up on top of the trunk. "What? Do you think I never thought about it? Out of the way humans, you made us, now let's see if I can make Angelina roar!"

The Birdman

Howard was a simple man that loved his animals, his wife, his son, and his province. Newfoundland had always held a special place in his heart. His grandfather and his father had taken him out to hunt moose, to ice fish, and when he had been old enough, to have his first beer down at the Legion. His daddy had shown him how to work a tractor, and his life had been filled with lots of good stuff. Howard sat on an old wooden chair behind his shed. It was a cold night in January, only just after five and it was already getting dark. *Shortest day of the year is passed*, he thought*, the days will get longer. A nice hot toddy made by Helen when I get in will hit the spot*. He unbuttoned his coat, just the top two buttons, so he could reach into his front shirt pocket. From there he took out a pinch of tobacco and dug his pipe out from his pants pocket with his left hand. He dropped the tobacco into the pipe's bowl, got out a match, and ran it along the side of the shed. The match burst into a small flame at the tip and he cupped his hand around the end of the pipe waiting a few seconds for the charcoal to burn off it. *Billy is a good boy*, he thought, *but he spends too much of his time on that cursed tablet. No wonder he's thirty years old, unmarried, and still* *living with us. Sure he could play baseball, even hockey when he was younger, but it never got him anywhere. He hasn't had a date in months that I know of and while I appreciate the help with the crops and the tractor since my back don't work like it used to, I wish he'd settle down. Man needs a woman to keep him straight, keep him out of mischief.* He puffed out smoke and made a ring with it, letting it drift through the air while a few snowflakes fell through it. His breath came out from his nose and the side of his mouth. Along with smoke from the pipe, it made a nice pattern, almost like some kind of engine. He saw headlights heading down the road, down Porter's Lane, which was just off Cherry Lane. He reached down to the grey wooden box at his feet. The hinges creaked just slightly as it opened and he reached in to get a small pair of black binoculars and a pencil. *Never hurts to be careful*, he thought, *that's what old granddad always said, 'course back here in the fifties, cars were unheard of—he told me it was 1961 before he even saw his first car.* That's when the writing had started, the collection of license plate numbers on the back of the shed. He looked up to the left, the first one was barely visible now, written over 50 years ago, the wind, rain, and ice had taken its toll on the shed. But he could still make out 'OO' and 'Happy' that brought a grin to his face.

Yeah those were the good old days, didn't have to get worry about being run over by some fool or a four-wheeler or a snow mobile. A fella could buy a drink or a pack of smokes if he could see over the counter. Best of all was the fishery; out on the water catching cod with dad and grandpa, getting paid in cash, there was no messing with regulations. Fuck, I never even knew what a life jacket was until I was twenty and some damned fool from the department of fisheries made us put one on.

He held the binoculars up to his eyes, the black leather strap falling behind his head, and waited for the car to pass. These days, cars would sometimes have a light just above the license plate, which made it easier to write it down. "HEL 882" he said aloud. *Damned new-fangled cars, what kind is that? I can't even hear the engine, must be one of those new electric ones I saw on the news. What's the bastard gonna do if the battery goes dead? Not much good if you're stuck in the snow somewhere, a gas can wouldn't do a lick of good.* He scratched the pencil on the wall. He had to bend over now; the numbers were down to his knees. His father had given up writing down the numbers, but Howard did it every night. It was a ritual. He had never been broken into, had never even had a stranger on the property that he knew of. But there was money in the shed, under the potatoes, and under the trap door. He wasn't about to give it to some bank. *A penny saved is a penny earned*, he thought, *and the way Helen spends, one of us sure has to.*

He put the binoculars and the pencils back in the box and got up. He put his hands behind his back to stretch it as he rose. *I'll be sixty-five in June, where has the time gone? Daddy always said the older you got, the quicker time goes by and it turns out he was right.* He took a few more puffs on his pipe and straightened up. Well, I should check out Blackie, Whitey, and Squawky; they haven't been fed since morning. Walking past the shed, he headed by the house and towards a large brown barn. *I never had much use for school*, he thought, *too busy fishing back then, and gave school up in grade ten. I do love that poem, "The Raven"; dad used to read it to me four or five nights a week at bed time. It's no wonder I wanted a raven when he passed and I inherited the house and property. The seagull and the crow, well they were fighting and damned near killed each other, only seemed right to help them recover, not like either of 'em would have made good eating.*

He got to the shed door, the hard packed snow and ice making crunching and squeaking noises under his boots, and took off the padlock. . "*Dummy locked*" Dad had called it, *not worth putting in a key and fastening it shut. With all the snow, ice, and rain we get here it would only rust shut.* The old extension cord was fed through a small gap on the right hand side of the door and was connected back to a plug on the back of the house. The gentle buzzing and whirring sounds of the space heaters greeted Howard as he entered, along with the bright red glow of one in the middle of the barn and one towards the back. The sound of the horse snorting and stomping along with a *moo*, reminded him of how the farm had dwindled over the years. *Used to have two cows, a bull, a horse, and a goat but people don't want fresh milk like they used to, and the horse is just too stubborn to die. He's been no use the past fifteen years since I finally got the tractor, and I just don't have the heart to shoot poor old Milly. Billy's going to have to work extra hours down at the supermarket. If he wants to stay in this house, he needs to help me pay the bills. Even the veggies don't sell like they used to, he chuckled to himself. Damned supermarkets sure don't make it easy for a local farmer to sell a few spuds or carrots these days. It's not Billy's fault, but he don't even realize he's part of the problem just working there.*

Howard petted Molly, scratching her head and putting some oats in her feed bucket. He put some hay down for the cow and headed over to the cages. A high-pitched "Hello," greeted him as he got close to Blackie's cage. A second later Squawky, the crow, responded with "Fuck you."

Howard laughed, *must have been Billy*, he thought. *He must come out here at night when I'm asleep, I've got to give the boy credit for having a sense of humor*. The seagull, Whitie, cried and Blackie chimed in again with "Hi". *No one can say I don't have a sense of humor, naming the crow squawky when he doesn't squawk at all*. Not to miss out, Squawky went "Caw-caw!" and jumped from one wooden perch in his cage to the other. The other two birds flapped their wings and shook their heads from side to side.

"Yes I know, you all want your feed. It's supper time for my feathered friends." He reached down and opened up a bag of bird seed on the floor. He kept it near the old space heater to keep it from getting moist. *Not too close though*, he thought, *wouldn't want to start a fire*. Opening the cages one by one, he gave them a few handfuls of feed. It had taken time, but after a year or so even the seagull would eat right from his hand.

Taking another puff from his pipe he said, "So what's the good word fellas?" Without fail, Blackie responded in his strange almost-strangled tone "Nevermore." He smiled once more, *that one's all mine, Billy won't listen to Poe anymore but I can count on the birds. Tomorrow morning might be a good time to read it again, keep the old brain in shape*. He glanced to the wall, his shotgun was held there just beyond the black metal cages. *Gun must be seventy years old now, grandpa looked after it and I do as well, tomorrow I'll give it a good clean*...his thoughts were interrupted as he heard a growl.

Turning quickly, he saw a huge wolf standing at the doorway to the shed. The redness of the space heater reflected in its eyes, giving it a demonic look.

"Well ain't that a sight for the eyes!" Howard shouted. *Forgot to close the door behind me, wind must have blown it open*. He was a big thing, way bigger than an average dog. His fur was a mixture of white and brown, and melting snow dripped from his fur onto the wooden floor. His teeth curled back to reveal white, sharp teeth and he growled once more. He moved forward and to the right, trying to get away from the heater and to get to the animals.

Howard felt the sweat break out on his forehead, his hands felt clammy and his mind raced. *Do I get out first? Release the animals? Push the heater towards him? Start yelling? No, I'll get this miserable vermin! I never hunted a wolf before, but I can still shoot*. Never taking his eye off of the wolf, he got his shotgun and opened up the barrels. *Two shots, I'm glad I kept it loaded. This must be one of those mutant wolf-coyote things I saw on the news, he's about to get a load of buckshot pumped into him!* The wolf edged forward, he was maybe twenty feet away now, his head lowered and his throat making a deep, guttural growl. The barrels made a *thunk* sound as he flicked them back into place, aimed, and fired. The heavy bang and small cloud of smoke came from the barrel. The wolf yipped, turned, and ran back out the door, knocking over the space heater he was next to.

Howard charged after him, leaving the door open to Blackie's cage, and bounded out the door. Helen was on the doorstep in her sealskin coat, slippers, and pajamas.

"Howard? Was that a gunshot? What's going on?" Her eyebrows were pressed together, concern on her face.

"Goddammit Helen, get back in the house! There's a wolf after the animals!" The wolf charged down the driveway and out towards the road. Howard aimed and fired, letting lose the last barrel. The wolf let out a strangled yipping sound, but bounded down the small hill and out of sight.

Helen screamed, "Wolf! Wolf! Billy, get down here right now!" and slammed the door. Howard slipped on ice beneath the snow and came down on his back, knocking the wind out of him for a few moments.

"Jesus Christ!" he yelled, "How stupid of me not to put down salt, lucky I didn't break my neck. At least the fucking thing is gone, hopefully I wounded the thing and it will bleed to death somewhere. I—" his voice was cut short as he heard the frantic neighing of Molly and the high pitched squawking of the birds. In the corner of his eye he saw Blackie fly off and land in a tree somewhere. "The heater! Helen! Billy!" he screamed, "Get out here with buckets, the barn is on fire!" He turned his head to the other side, getting to one knee and then painfully standing, dropping his shotgun to the ground. Flames licked out from the door and smoke began to billow out from the sides.

Howard ran to the extension cord and unplugged it from the house, then searched frantically for the hose. Finding the knob he tried to turn it, but his hands slipped, it was covered with ice. *Where are Helen and Billy?* As if summoning them, they both ran out the front door. Billy was in his underwear with a t-shirt and boots on, they both had buckets of water and ran towards the shed and flicked them at the door. "Wait! The fire is inside for now, go get some more water, hurry!" He managed to kick the door open with his foot and got inside. The flames pushed him back, all the dry hay and the old space heater made for a terrible combination. He took off his coat and wrapped it around his hands, determined to save some of the animals. He immediately started to cough from the smoke and fumbling, managed to open the doors to the bird cages. Helen and Billy showed up then and flicked water inside the barn. They managed to douse him but did little to stop the fire. "Get out of here!" Howard yelled before descending into a coughing fit, "Go call the fire department!" Helen put her arm around Howard and helped him out. Billy had started to cough and stumbled out himself.

Howard collapsed to the ground choking, Helen dug out her cell phone from her pocket and hit three buttons. "Yes...we have a fire, 42 Porter's Lane. Get a fire truck here right away!" Her voice cracked and tears spilled from her eyes, the phone slipped from her hand and fell into the snow. Tears sprung to his eyes as he heard the cow frantically mooing and poor Molly made an awful scream. Billy, showing more courage than he gave him credit for, returned with a pair of gloves and another full water bucket. Before they could stop him he was back in the barn, the water splashed as his hands blistered.

"Ah Jesus, my hands!" Billy quickly blindfolded Molly and dragged her from the barn. Molly's tail was on fire and Billy grabbed it with his hands, desperate to pat out the fire.

The smoke continued to come from the shed as the flames came through the doors and the windows shattered. *The shells were old, he thought, maybe fifty years or more, left over from grandpa. They didn't have the range they should of, just another sign that I'm getting sloppy!* Sirens could be heard in the distance but Howard knew it was too late for the cow, too late for his farm, maybe too late for anything ever again. His eyes closed as he slipped into unconsciousness.

☐

Funny Tricks

Mike looked out the window. The snow lazily drifted down to the ground as it slowly added to the blanket of white that covered the driveway. He was at his kitchen table, sipping on his coffee and he thought, *It's 3:00 a.m., I just lost four-hundred bucks at poker, and I don't have to be at work 'till 4:00 p.m., but screw it. This coffee has me wired and I can't let winter get me down. I'll head out for a walk.*

He lived in Newfoundland, an island in the middle of the North Atlantic Ocean, and it was turning out to be a bad winter. Over two hundred centimeters of snow had fallen since December, and this was only mid-January. A walk would be good. He could use the exercise, the holidays were always bad. Drinking, over-eating, and his cousin's wedding had put him over two hundred pounds now. Not that he had anyone to impress, his hair was grey and mostly gone, and at forty he was almost at the point of giving up looking for a girlfriend.

His house was small, just one bedroom with no basement, but it's not like he needed much space. His cat was some company, he smiled to himself, *Cat, not much of a name, but it's simple and easy to remember*. The rent was small and so far he had been managing to pay it. As he walked, the snow continued to drift down around him. It landed on his head and made him blink as some touched his eyelashes. He continued down Cherry Lane, heading left toward Martha's Place, which would bring him down to Manuels River and the trail. The snow made alternating crunching and squeaking sounds as he walked. His breath puffed out in front of him. There was no one around this early in the morning, and that was the way he liked it. Taking out his phone, he checked to see what movies would be out this weekend. *Another Saturday night alone, he thought, I'll have to sneak some beer in to drown my sorrows.* His concentration was broken when he heard "Hello" from somewhere nearby. Mike jumped back, almost dropping his phone and whipped his head around.

"What the fuck? Ah, hello? Anyone there?"

Turning his head this way and that, he scanned the area around him. He had just started to walk down the steps between two houses that lead down to the river. He couldn't see anyone, just trees and snow. This time he heard "Hi," and it was high-pitched, like a little kid might sound, or girl.

"Ok whoever this is, knock it off. I'm not impressed, and I'm in no mood to be screwed with." Not willing to let this person get the better of him, he flicked the screen on the phone and hit the flashlight button. He scanned around with the light and found a bird, a crow he thought, just sitting on a branch, looking at him.

This time he heard it distinctly: "Fuck you." Again he started, stepping back a bit and slipping off of the wooden stair.

"Ah, shit!" he called out, not hurt but just wet and pissed off. "Seriously?" Mike responded, "A crow just said 'fuck you' to me?" He looked around and the bird was gone. He shook his head, dusted himself off, and kept going. *That was some weird shit*, he thought, *I watched that episode of* The Simpsons *with the Edgar Allan Poe story in it just the other night.*

He heard from above him and off to the side, "Nevermore!" as if the bird had known his thoughts.

"Jesus!" he shouted. His heart was pounding in his chest, "What is going on here? Some bird out to get me?" He quickly made a snowball and threw it in the direction that the voice had come from. Only the noise of a gentle *thump* greeted him as it hit a tree. He shrugged his shoulders and continued, *What the hell is going on tonight? It's all I need. The boss says I need to be better at transcribing, I haven't been laid in months, and now some raven or crow is fucking with me!* Not seeing any choice, he was already past the half-way point on the flight of stairs that would lead down or back up to the road, he continued down towards the river. He kicked some snow and put his head down. He played with his phone some more, bringing up a funny video to watch on YouTube. He started to calm down, let go of a few chuckles watching a man fall into a pond, and another of a guy getting pushed into a pool. Soon though, he noticed that his breath was no longer puffing out in front of him, and that some fog had drifted in as a he crossed a bridge over Manuels River. That by itself wasn't so strange, the weather could change in Newfoundland quickly and fog was a regular occurrence, even in winter.

Then he heard it; a bark from behind him that made him drop his phone. Quickly stopping, he retrieved it and spun about. A coyote stood on the bridge not ten feet behind him. Now his mind started to race, *Fuck! fuck! fuck! What do I do? Do you run from coyotes? Back away slowly? Make noise and raise your arms? I don't remember.* It looked big, maybe 100 pounds. His fur was white and brown, some snow was on his head, and he flicked it like a dog to clear it off. Mike had heard about some freaky wolf-coyote hybrids that were in Labrador, but he hadn't known that they had made it to the island yet. Mike felt his heart pounding again, and his throat tightened. *I'm a lot bigger than him, coyotes only attack small animals and children, I think.*

It let out another bark, "Yip! Yip! A-oooo!" The howl raised the hairs on the back on Mike's neck. *I'm backing up, I've got to get out of here before anything else crazy happens or some other coyotes show up to answer his call.* Slowly, he backed away. The coyote-animal looked at him again and then bounded back across the bridge and out of sight.

Once it was gone, Mike turned and ran. *I can't take any more of this tonight!* he thought, *I have to get back to the house and get a drink, something to settle my nerves!* Being 240 pounds and not doing more than a walk a few times a week didn't give him much stamina. He made it up the first five steps of another set of stairs, this one leading back up to the road. He stopped, wheezing and out of breath. With his hands on his knees, he looked to the side. Manuels River rushed by beside him, it never got cold enough here for it freeze over. The water helped to sooth his rattled mind and he calmed his breathing, taking deep breathes and wiping his forehead with the back of his hand. The sweat ran down his back and made him both hot and cold at the same time. Standing back up, he turned around. There was no coyote behind him, and turning again in place, he couldn't spot any raven or crow either. He let out another long, slow breath and continued. *Just some strange stuff tonight, nothing to worry about.* Holding down the button on his phone, he said "Play Don't Worry Be Happy, by Bobby McFerrin." Siri did as he asked and he trudged up the stairs, feeling a little better.

Here's a little song I wrote
You might want to sing it note for note
Don't worry, be happy.

Mike walked up the newly finished stone steps, past a doggie bag station, and finally into the parking lot. He sang along a little with the song, still catching his breath, but coming around. *Got to do more cardio*, he thought, *that's what they said in Zombieland*. He looked over at the sign that said MANUELS RIVER TRAIL LINEAR PARK, underneath which, it said FOSSIL SITE. *Fossils, I remember taking one when I was a kid and the teacher brought us down here for a field trip. I wonder if that's worth anything*. Suddenly a black cat ran from behind some bushes and crossed in front of him, disappearing back down the steps and letting out a strangled "Meow!" just as quickly as it had come. Mike dropped his phone in the snow and shook his fist in the air.

"God damn it! It's like everything tonight is out to get me! Little bastard, good thing I don't believe in any of that superstitious crap." He was too tired to chase after it. Picking up his phone, he brushed off the snow and put it in his pocket, making a mental note to take the Otterbox case off of it when got back to dry it out. *Well I didn't believe it. Today is Friday the thirteenth, and I've got to say it's been one weird, unlucky day for me so far. Lost at online poker at home, tripped up in a cord going out the door, and of course all the damned weird freaky shit on the walk!* Mike thought about the other things that were unlucky, walking under a ladder, leaving from a different door than the one you came in, breaking a mirror…as if on cue he heard a *crunch*. Looking down he saw that someone had left pieces of a mirror on the sidewalk. Shrugging his shoulders he thought, *the last seven years sucked, can't see why the next would be much different.* He knew that the meaning of Friday the thirteenth had to do with the Bible; thirteen apostles and the crucifixion on a Friday. His parents had made him go to church until he had been fourteen, weird how some stuff sticks with you. He thought of how buildings didn't have a number thirteen button in elevators, *weird old crap, I don't buy it. Tonight has been fucked up, the weirdest walk I've ever had, but still, shit happens.*

Making his way past the Irving station, he thought of a few nights ago. *Christina's wedding was fun, open bar, good looking women, getting to see my American cousins for the first time in fourteen years, the photo booth where you could put on masks. Of course the best part was when that woman at the bar said I smelled good. Why didn't I ask for her number? It sucks still being this shy, all I could do was mutter "thanks" and get another beer.* Kicking the snow and putting his head down, he passed by Berg's Famous Ice Cream. The sign read CLOSED FOR THE SEASON. *That's the way I feel*, he thought, *except my love life seems to be closed permanently.* He turned up Cherry Lane, passing Elle Salon and Booster Juice. *Every day is just one day*, he thought. *Today was crappy, but tomorrow will be better. After work I can go see Rogue One again, maybe go to the Bella Vista and play some poker. I just need to get off my ass and get rid of this spare tire. Sara is always saying that she would go walking with me and it would be nice to have some company.*

The sound of a horn went off from inside Mike's pocket. *It does sound like something from Robin Hood,* he thought. His friends and co-workers had often commented on it, teasing him a little. He dug his phone out and had a look; the screen displayed (780) 560-7750. *Funny, I don't know that number at all,* he thought, *maybe a telemarketer?* Stopping in front of the former Police Station on the right, he took his gloves off and unlocked the phone.

The text read, *Hi Mike, it's Andy. The bar just shut down, I'm nearby, want to have a drink at your place? I got a flask!* Mike smiled. Andy was his cousin from Boston. *He did always like a drink, and after all this weird shit, fuck it, I can have a drink with him, especially if he's bringing it.*

He replied: *Sure Andy, I'll be home in a few minutes. See ya soo-*

As his fingers hit the black button at the bottom of his phone, a pickup truck came hurtling up Cherry Lane. It was a GMC 1500 with extra-large snow tires, coal black, with barely enough snow cleared on the windshield to see. Mike didn't have time to react, to move. The tires slipped on a small patch of ice going into the parking lot. The driver's head slumped down on his shoulder and his eyes closed. There was a sickening *thump* as Mike's head hit the truck's grill and his body was slammed to the ground. His fingers twitched a final time and he glanced up. He recognized the driver as Andy, who stumbled out of the truck and fell to his knees. Blood ran down into Mike's eyes and the world went black.

☐

From a Spark to a Flame

A blazing fire roared in the fireplace. It was a cold winter day at the Radik Castle, and while the fire helped, Valere wrapped her woolen shawl around her shoulders as she stood in front of the hearth. Behind her sat Vincent, engrossed in a book. He was ten now and was such a curious boy. He had read through everything in the library, and any book relating to dragons he had read at least three times. Valere was soon overtaken by a fit of coughing. Since she had turned sixty they had only gotten worse. "Vin—" she stopped to clear her failing voice, "Ahem. Vincent, be a good boy and fetch your Nan some water. Frog stuck in my throat."

Vincent put down his book. This one had a red leather-bound cover and was entitled *Zat-Kaz Tales of Joy and Sorrow along the Blade Coast*. It made a heavy *thud* as it hit the floor. "Okay Nanna, I'll be right back." Vincent ran into the other room, he was quick on his head and jumped over the dog lying prostrate in front of the door.

Valere held her fist in front of her face "Ah. Ahem," this was her second fit today, better than yesterday, but it still troubled her. Her son, Pivan, should have paid for a priest to come here. A simple healing spell or at the very least someone knowledgeable in medicine might clear it up. But no, Piven spent most of his time now at parties. He was always trying to keep up the Radik image, and of course gamble with the other Lords.

She heard Vincent call out from down the hall, "Patrick! Get up here now, and bring some water!" There was the *ding-ding-ding* sound of a bell—one was kept on every table throughout the house. Vincent was dependent on the staff, and she tried to teach him to show them respect, but it was all for naught once Piven got home. After losing at gambling, he'd often find some tiny mistake the maid had done. If she missed a spot of dirt on the floor, or forgot to dust a cabinet, he'd give her a proper tongue-lashing. It wasn't right for Vincent to repeat what his father said, and to also treat all the servants less like people, and more like slaves. She would apologize to poor Nina when no one was around, but the poor thing would always be in tears. Valere used to bring it up to Piven but she just didn't have the energy to fight with him anymore.

Things had been different when Oth had been alive, but that had been five years ago. Damned fool should have never gone, but when he heard about the treasure that the black dragon had, well, he had his staff and golden dagger out before you could shake a stick. They had beaten the dragon. Oth had done one of his wonderful incantations and had hit it with a huge burst of fire, but the dragon's death throes had managed to finish off most of the group, including Oth. Valere let out another small cough and saw Patrick come into the room. He awkwardly bowed with the water jug, glasses, and tray balanced on his hands. "Lady Radik, Master Vincent said that you need some water."

Valere stood and came over to Patrick. "I told you to stop bowing, Patrick. You have been with the family now for over twenty years, I consider you a friend more than any—" before she could continue, Vincent bounded in the room. "Not bowing Nanna? Surely, you don't mean it. Daddy says that servants must always know their place." Patrick handed her the glass and she took it, taking big gulps of the water. Then she sat back down. Patrick filled up the other glass and laid it on the side table next to the chair where Valere had sat.

"Master Vincent is correct, Lady Radik, everyone has their place in this world. Mine is to serve, never-the-less, I do appreciate the sentiment. Would you like some hot tea to soothe your throat milady?"

Valere nodded, "That would be wonderful Patrick, my thanks. These old bones don't stay warm like they used to, not on such a cold winter's day."

Vincent took the other glass and drank the water. "I could use some toast and jam Patrick, and don't take too long, Nanna and I don't like to be kept waiting."

Putting the tray under his arm, Patrick bowed to the young boy, "Of course, Master Vincent, I will instruct the cook to make haste."

Valere finished off the glass of water and looked to Vincent. He was growing fast; he was already five feet tall. His red hair slipped down in front of his eyes and he brushed it away with his hand. All the red bumps on his skin, almost like scales, were an indication of what her father-in-law, his great grandfather, had done. *It is something of a family secret*, she thought, *but he will discover it soon enough. Perhaps it is time to tell him.* "Come and see your nanna, your book will still be there afterwards. I have something important to tell you."

Vincent came over to the chair and climbed up in his nanna's lap. He looked towards the fire, staring at it intensely. "You have always loved fire, haven't you, my boy? It's time that you knew why."

He turned back to face her, "I love to watch things burn. This morning I threw a bug in the fire, just to watch it turn to ash." Valere took Vincent's face between her palms and looked into his eyes.

"You must be careful with fire Vincent, it is not a toy. Bugs too have a place in the world. Don't do that again, promise me?

Vincent let out a sigh, "Ok, I promise, can you tell me the story now? I have to do my math and history with Mommy in a little while."

Valere pulled the red woolen shawl down on her shoulders, careful not to knock Vincent off her lap. *Even with the fire it's so hard to stay warm*, she thought. "You know that the world is a magical place; there are priests who can cast spells with their faith, and wizards and sorcerers who can do the same with study and practice. Dragons, ogres, unicorns, elves and all sorts of other wonderful creatures exist, too. As you know, your grandfather could use magic. He had a magic cloak and ring, among other fantastic items."

Vincent had been staring into the fire again but turned back, rolling his eyes. "I know, Nanna, I read two books about all that last week."

Valere frowned, "You have a need to be careful of your manners, Vincent. Not everyone will be as patient as I. As I was saying, this happened a long time ago, way before you were born. Your great-grandfather Victor, who also knew a thing or two about the arcane—that's the magic that doesn't come from faith—met a beautiful woman in the forest. She was an elf with long silver hair that was on patrol for her king. Well, one thing led to another, and Victor and this elf, Elianna, fell in love. Then one day your grandfather was born."

Vincent squirmed in her lap, "Nanna, I knew that, you told me that lots of times! They had Oth in the spring, and he became a great sorcerer." His eyes returned to the fire as she put her arms around him, holding his hands in hers.

"I'm getting there, Vincent," she said, "My old mind doesn't work as fast as it used to. Be patient. So Oth had red bumps on his skin, like you do, and he loved fire. They caught him outside setting fire to the grass, and he almost burned down the shed outside the estate more than once." Vincent saw her eyes flick to the box on the couch. "Be a dear and go over and get the silver box, there's something inside it for you."

Vincent got up and fetched it. "I could never get in this box, it is always locked. I never burned the grass or the shed, Nanna, but even if I did the servants would build another one, it's their job."

Valere reached into her dress and pulled up a necklace with a key on it. "You were never a good listener, Vincent. treat everyone at this house with respect. The box is locked because it holds something important, a figurine that has been in our family for over eighty years now." Vincent handed her the box and she put the key in. The box made a gentle creaking sound as it opened.

Inside was a red dragon figurine about eight inches tall that lay on its side. Valere took it out of the box and held it in front of Vincent. "It turns out that your great-grandmother Elianna wasn't an elf at all, but a red dragon. You see, dragons are able to change their shape to appear as other animals, a person, or an elf."

Vincent's eyes opened wide as the fire reflected off the red surface of the statue. The base of the statue was made of silver like the coins his dad had shown him. The eyes were tiny diamonds that sparkled in the firelight. It was old; the base had a little black tarnish from the years, but was otherwise spotless and looked like it was worth thousands of gold, maybe more. "Can I hold it, Nanna? I promise I'll be careful."

She nodded as her eyes filled up, the tears threatening to brim over. "Oth gave this to me just before he went out on his last adventure to kill Green Death. The black dragon finished him though, and this is all I have left of him."

Vincent took it carefully and turned it end over end in his hands. he held it up to the fire and noticed once more how the light reflected upon it. He ran his fingers over it, admiring the detail and the craftsmanship of the figurine. "I give it to you now, Vincent. Treasure it and think of your grandfather and his father. It is a part of our family history, and it signifies what you may already have felt in your heart. The call to dragons, the love of fire, and the spark of magic that I know is in you." Tears spilled out over her eyelashes and fell to her cheeks.

"But Nanna, red dragons are evil. That's what it said in the book I read. Why would she be with great-granddad? Does that mean that I'm evil, or my dad is?" His eyes were wide and his mouth hung open. He scratched at his chin and tilted his head to one side, peering at her intently.

Valere dabbed at her eyes and held out her hands. She pulled him in for a hug. "Dragons do strange things sometimes. Maybe Elianna wasn't all bad? Maybe not all red dragons are evil? We'll never know for sure. Don't see everything as black and white, Vincent, most everything and everyone is a shade of grey. You're not evil, my sweet boy." She kissed him on the top of his head, "Don't let magic or money or anything else consume you. Remember your friends and your family, they are important. Now put another log on the fire for your Nanna, I just can't get warm today."

Vincent looked up and nodded. "I'll remember, Nanna, and I do know what you mean. Last night I made a book float in the air, let me show you what else I can do."

Valere's eyes opened wide, *I knew he had the talent; it's in our blood, but so soon? I hope he knows what's he's doing.* "Be careful now, Vincent, fire is not a toy." As she watched, Vincent picked up the iron poker and rubbed some soot from it onto his hands, and put in on the floor. Then he picked up a piece of wood lying in a box by the fireplace and picked off a few tiny pieces of bark with his fingernails. They were little slivers no bigger than his thumb. He rubbed two pieces of thumb-sized bark together in his hands, took a step back from the fireplace, and began to chant. Vincent's hands made circles as he said, "Heka ropn aanbaktm kirkampia!" at the end he pointed three fingers of each hand toward the fire and blew the remaining soot from his hands.

The fire roared and blazed hotter and bigger than ever. The chair Valere was sitting on began to singe, "Vincent! The fire, what have you done? Oh, no!" before she had a chance to push the chair back, the hem of her dress was aflame! Vincent charged forward and dumped the remaining water on her, putting the flames out. In her effort to get out of the chair, she pushed too hard and the older furniture fell backwards and hit the floor with a heavy *thump* and small *crack*, Valere winced in pain as her elbow hit the ground.

Vincent moved forward and looked into his nanna's face, his eyes now starting to brim with tears. "Nanna, I'm sorry! Are you burned? Are you hurt? I only wanted to make you warmer."

She closed her eyes and rubbed her neck, then her elbow. "I'll be all right, Vincent, help Nanna out of the chair and do your spell again, only this time in reverse. Make the fire smaller before you burn the place down!" Vincent carefully pulled her from the chair and she sat up on the floor. Vincent saw that his nanna was right, the fire burned so hot now that the box in front of it was starting to smolder, as was the carpet. Luckily, the poker had been left further away. He gathered up the soot and the fallen wood chips, and chanted and gestured once more.

☐

Footprints Part 1

Marlon bolted up in the bed. His heart was pounding, his face was flushed, and sweat glistened on his face. "No! Keep away from me!" Marlon blurted out, his eyes still closed, his arms thrashing about. He hit the man next to him in the chest.

"What the hell, Marlon? That hurt!" He had long red hair that hung around his head like a shaggy mane and his beard reached down to his collarbone.

Marlon opened his eyes, took a deep breath and turned his head. "Sorry, Larry, bad dreams again. Did I hurt you?" Larry also let out a long breath, rubbed his chest and took Marlon's hand. "You know I'm a lot tougher than that. What had you so upset? Was it the war again?"

Marlon let him hold his hand and nodded. "I...thank you for asking, but I just need some time. I'm going outside for a smoke." Larry let him go.

"I might be a simple woodsman, but I can still listen. I hope sometime soon you'll open up about this. It's not good to keep all this to yourself. I can see what it's doing to you."

Marlon pulled on his pants and shirt, sliding his feet into woolen slippers that rested beside the bed. "Not now. Ok, Lar? You don't know how horrible it was. I...some of them were just kids." Larry sat up in bed and then stood up, reaching for Marlon.

"I only want to hel-" but Marlon strode out the door and went towards the kitchen. It was almost dawn and some light came in from the windows. Marlon shivered as the sweat began to dry on his face and back. He went to the lantern on the kitchen table and took out a match from the box beside it. Pushing the pump about thirty times, he then dragged the match against the old cedar table and stuck it up inside the glass top, holding it to the cloth wick. The lantern lit and began to put out a double white glow. He went to the sink and opened a drawer to the left of it and fished out the pack of Lucky Strike cigarettes. Larry had given him a pipe for his birthday, but these were so much easier. Grabbing the pack of matches, he stuffed them in one pocket, and found his coat and his rifle where they hung from a nail to the right side of the door. He slung the strap over his right shoulder. *Can't be too careful*, he thought, *never been attacked by a bear yet, but it's mid-June and mating season for grizzlies*. He opened the bolt, made sure it was still loaded, and slammed it back in place. He slid the door's metal bar to the left, carefully trying not to wake Larry. *He's a dear, but he'll go back to sleep. All that hunting yesterday wore him out.*

He set the lantern on the steps and tapped the pack of cigs, getting a fresh one out. Mist rose from the ground and fog hung low in the air as he glanced up at the forest all around him. He put the cigarette between his lips and had another look around, finally laying the rifle on the top step beside him. *All clear, that's what Sergeant Wilson used to say, poor bastard, fat lot of good it did 'im.* Only a small dirt trail led the way back to the road and the town of Juneau; it was a good hour walk back to town. He dug out a match and dragged it across the back of the pack. Cupping his hand around his face, he held the match to the end of the cig and lit it. Taking a long drag, he exhaled, the smoke making puffs from his two nostrils and his mouth. Even in mid-June it was still chilly and Marlon hugged himself inside his jacket. *Florida sure is warmer*, he thought, *but Alaska has its charms; the northern lights, peace and quiet, lots of different animals, and of course, Larry.* Taking in a deep breath, he slowly let it back out. *They are getting less frequent; this is only my second night terror this month. That's a lot better than one every three or four nights a week.* He listened for the sounds that comforted him. An owl let out a few final hoots and a wolf could be heard howling somewhere in the distance. Birds had started chirping, and he spotted a moose about one hundred yards away. It was just leaving the tree line, out for a morning stroll.

He took another draw from his cigarette and felt the tension start to leave his shoulders. *I wonder how Ma and Da are doing. Haven't seen or heard from them in almost a year now. Much as love the quiet, it might be time to head to Saint Augustine. Winter would be a good time to get out of here, and maybe Larry could even come with me. I'd have to lie of course, say he worked for the newspaper or some such thing.*

Marlon looked around. The moose paid him little attention, just gnawed on leaves and berries. I've got plenty of pictures of moose, he thought, the bastard would make good eating though. He reached down for his rifle. He had been shooting since he was twelve, and with over thirty years of practice, he could take it out from here easily. Feeling the cold steel of the barrel in his left hand, he hesitated. *No, not now*, he thought, *I don't want to wake Larry, and there is still half a caribou in the freezer*. He took another drag on his cigarette and tapped the ash off on the ground. He reached in his pocket and pulled out a letter. It was from his old war buddy, Gary Lock. A nice fella, and the only person he had kept in contact with since the war. *Gary is a great guy*, he thought, *never judged me, was always handy in a fight, and knew the truth. The dead were a lot more lively in France, had to put the bastards in the ground again*. He put his finger in the corner of the envelope, tore it, and then dragged his finger across slowly, tearing it but not the paper inside. The letter had been here for weeks, but Larry respected his privacy and had never touched it. He hadn't even asked about it. A part of Marlon didn't want to read it; he suspected what it could contain. Sure they chatted about work, about what they had both done after the war, but while Gary had continued to work with the government, Marlon had left that life. Hell, he was almost a hermit up here, except for Larry and the hunting trips, of course. Marlon's photography made them some money but not enough for both of them to live off of. He didn't mind the guide work, it often gave him the opportunity for some great shots, and it wasn't good to be cooped up in the cabin with Larry all the time. He smiled again, it wasn't that the two of them weren't entertained, but he wasn't as young as he used to be, and more than twice a day was tough now, even if they took turns pitching and catching.

He started to read the letter. The sun was rising over the long grass, and he turned off the lamp.

Dear Marlon,
I hope this letter finds you well. I enjoyed reading your last letter. I understand that you miss being with the boys, the army did provide a wonderful brotherly bond, and I miss it sometimes too.

Marlon stopped reading and laughed, *that's not what I meant Gary. I clearly said that I'm with Larry and I enjoy men, but perhaps it's for the best. I know you and the rest of the troop wouldn't understand. Hell, I supposed we could be arrested if the wrong person found out.* He glanced up once, scanned around and noticed that the moose was gone. Old habits die hard; have to be sure the area is clear. His eyes returned to where he had left off in the letter.

I was back home in New York for a while. Marlene and me had a kid, Abigail. She's a joy, Marlon, you'd love her. Well, with another mouth to feed, I found we were stretched thin on a patrolman's salary. So when the army contacted me and said there was some bad hombre in Mexico we had to deal with, the pay was just too good for me to say no.

Marlon took one final big drag on his cigarette, tapped off the rest of the ashes and tossed it into the trees. Larry wouldn't like it, but Marlon didn't give a crap. The ground was still dewy and it wasn't like it would start a fire.

The mission started off normal enough. We met with our contact in a village and he told us how some crazy bandits had come into town. They had taken all the women, killed most of the men, and had tried to burn the whole place down. The few Mexican army men with us decided to stay in the town. It was just us and this old grizzled guide that went out to look for these bastards.

Marlon glanced around and listened. Birds chirped and a wolf howled in the distance. *Larry, and pop trained me well*, he thought, *he's at least a mile off and it's most likely just because it's sunrise.*

He returned to the letter once more as a few streams of sunlight made their way down the trees, one of them illuminated the paper.

We headed out into the mountains. I'll tell you buddy, even though we were far south, it got cold up there. Not like the trenches, but still, I was glad I wore my long johns. Anyway, we got out of the mountains and found this abandoned camp. It brought me back to the war; bodies were torn to pieces, blood was everywhere. The guide turned wide, tossed his cookies, and high-tailed it out of there. We didn't bother to stop 'im. I wanted to turn back then but Smythe and the boys wouldn't hear of it. Parsons found some tracks and we continued on. Wasn't long before we found the bandits, well most of 'em, the leader wasn't among the bodies. No sooner had we decided to bring back the bandit leader's body—he had the biggest gun on 'im and was mostly in one piece—then Parsons spotted something. It was some kind of corpse tied to on a wooden platform. Once we got close enough, we saw the poor bastard had been killed and then just left there, I'd say for years. His skin was like leather from the wind and sand, and his face was sunken in and his nose was gone. Me and parsons climbed up

the platform to cut the sad sack down. No sooner did we have the ropes off him and his hands pulled free then he made the most horrible moaning sound and he tried to strangle me! Things only went from bad to worse. The old bandit leader wasn't so dead after all neither, despite his guts being around his ankles. He started after Smythe with a knife. 'Fore we knew it some Native People who should've been dead came up over the horizon and tried to do us in. If all that wasn't bad enough, up outta the sand came the biggest goddamned snake I ever laid eyes on! Fucker must'a been twenty feet long and moved like a whip. Luckily, we was all armed to the teeth, but still it killed two of the boys and finished off the bad hombre, swallowed him whole he did! We somehow made it out of that godforsaken country and back to the city. I got my pay and was told to keep my trap shut; you remember the way it was after France. Look after yerself, Marlon, me and Smythe miss yeh. Look me up you ever make to the big apple.
Your pal,
Gary

The letter had been shaking in Marlon's hand for a good minute and he finally let it fall to the ground. Tears streamed down from his eyes and he put his hands up to his face. He let a sob escape his lips and said aloud, "Dear God. The dead again, I can't go see him. They just wouldn't fall down, they kept standing up." The door opened behind him and he turned to see Larry standing there with his tweed shirt and stained brown trousers in the door way. Two steaming cups occupied his hands. The smile on his face quickly turned to a frown as he sat down beside Marlon on the steps, laying the cup behind him.

"The war again, honey? Did I hear you say they kept standing up?" He leaned in and kissed Marlon's forehead and pulled him in for a hug. Larry's hands rubbed the small of Marlon's back.

Marlon whispered in his ear, "I...I never told you everything. It wasn't just the shells and the Germans and the cold, there was...I'm sorry, love, I'm still not ready, but thank you. I am doing better, less bad dreams. It was just this letter from my old army buddy, Gary, he brought it all back, not his fault." He didn't like to lie to Larry, but it was so horrible during the war and what he said wasn't even much of a lie.

Larry gently pushed him back. Reaching up, he wiped away the tears from Marlon's eyes and kissed him on the forehead. "I know, Mar, it's something you'll always carry with you. You'll tell me when it's time. Gary, huh? He someone who kept you warm before you met me? Here, drink your coffee." Larry handed him a cup and Marlon took it, cradling it in his hands and breathing the vapors in deep. He took a sip, laid it down and punched Larry in the arm playfully.

"No, silly! It wasn't like that with me and Gary, it wasn't like that with me and anyone before you. Thanks for the cup and the company, I like to be alone but I was ready for a break."

Larry smiled and rubbed his shoulder, "You still know how to throw a punch! And the coffee was my pleasure. Say, how about we walk into town for some breakfast? I know you're probably tired of eggs and hard tack, plus I did see the check you laid out on the table, those shots from a month ago paid off well."

Marlon took another sip and held the cup again. The warmness was pleasant in his hands. "Aren't you eagle-eyed? Yes, old George at the Augustine Tribute has always been a fan of my work, and that herd of caribou was beautiful, we were lucky to find them. Sure let's go into town for a bite. I'd like to take our hunting gear though. Afterwards, can we go for a hike? Maybe shoot some buffalo?"

Larry took a long sip of coffee and scrunched up his face, looking at Marlon with one eye. "Buffalo? Are you sure, hon? They are fast buggers and hard to catch. Hell, I haven't seen one in months. They ain't so plentiful these days."

Marlon laid his hand on Larry's shoulder, putting his coffee aside. "Please Lar, you know that a hunt clears my head and calms me. I'll take my camera, if we do spot them I'll get some shots first. We don't need to kill them all, besides I've never had buffalo meat and you're such a good cook."

Larry laughed and then kissed Marlon on the lips. His eyes twinkled and Marlon smiled. "It's Hard to say no to anyone that cute. All right, then. Get your gear, have a shave, and we'll move out. Remember, I'm the hairy one, I like you dolphin smooth."

Marlon coughed and spit out the last bit of coffee he was drinking. "Ah-hem! Don't push your luck, you're good with a razor but there're some places I don't want that anywhere near! Thanks though, and I would like you to teach me more about tracking."

* * *

Marlon followed closely behind Larry. They walked through the tall grass that came up past their waists, almost completely concealing them as they hunched over.

"The key is to see how fresh the tracks are." Larry whispered, "And also the dung. If it's soft, you know it's fresh and they can't be far ahead."

Marlon made a gagging sound and whispered back, "That mean's touching it, I assume."

"Yeah, to be sure I usually do."

"Do you need to smell it as well?"

"No, you don't need to smell it."

"How do you tell the difference between a buffalo print and say a moose or caribou?"

Larry turned back towards Marlon, "That's a good question; they all have cloven hooves, so they look split apart. Moose tracks are more heart-shaped, caribou and buffalo are more ovular. Now get your camera out, they are big bastards, but they can run if they want to."

There was movement up ahead. Larry stopped and held up his hand and Marlon halted. He pulled the camera up from the strap around his neck, took off the lens cap and held it up to his eye, straightening up just a little bit.

About four hundred feet away was a big buffalo. It stamped its foot and snorted, looked around, and then went back to munching grass. Larry took out his rifle and bullets.

"Take a few shots, just be careful. I'll move to the right so I can shoot clearly if needed." Marlon nodded and stood to his full height. He started to snap off some pics, remembering to wind the camera each time, and stepped forward. The buffalo had brown shaggy fur all over it. Some twigs stuck in the fur and two small white horns protruded on either side of its head.

How can he even see? Marlon thought, *the fur almost covers his eyes.* He crept closer, lifting one foot up slowly and carefully putting it back down. In his light brown jacket, pants, and boots, he wasn't easy to spot, especially as the beast just kept eating with its head down. *These should be some good ones,* he thought, *I haven't sent Gerry a buffalo spread in years, might even take one after it's dead in case he wants to do a hunting piece.* The buffalo glanced at him but turned its big shaggy head back down, continuing to munch up and swallow grass.

Marlon was maybe two hundred feet away and he heard the soft *ch-chunk* sound that he knew was Larry putting a bullet into his rifle. *One more shot*, he thought, this time he stood straight up and the buffalo stared right at him. His dark brown eyes locked with Marlon's green ones for a split second and he took the picture. He heard Larry call out, "That's close enough, hon. Get down!" The buffalo's eyes darted back and forth, finally getting a sense of the danger and it started to charge! Marlon knew the routine, dropped to his knees and watched as the shot whizzed by to his right and struck the beast on the right horn. Bits of it blew off, exploding into the air like bark from a tree. The animal let out an ear-splitting grunt of pain and surprise, Marlon's army training immediately kicked in. His had his rifle in his hand in a split second, the bullet in it in the next, and was aiming his shot. A second bullet whizzed through the air, this one he felt pass over the top of his head. "Jesus Christ, Larry, that was close!" he yelled. The bullet struck the buffalo on the other side of its head, once again striking it in the horn and making an explosion of white bone. The beast was close now, less than a hundred feet from Marlon. It only stopped for a second, reeling more from shock than pain, and continued forward.

Larry yelled back, "it's moving too fast! Take it down, now!" Marlon could hear the concern in

Larry's voice; he knew that Larry was in tears or at least on the verge. Marlon was cool under fire, he was confident in his shooting ability, but this was a tricky shot. He had to hit it right in the eye to make sure it would die instantly. He held the scope to his eye and took in a breath. He held it and then exhaled, pulling the trigger at the same time. The bullet tore through the air with a mighty *thung.* As the beast was virtually on top of him, the round went right into its left eye. The jelly from the eyeball exploded outwards along with blood and tissue. Marlon tumbled to the right with the rifle. The buffalo let out a grunt of pain as it faltered, skidded, and finally fell to the ground not two feet from where Marlon had been.

Blood began to pool around the beast's head, soaking into the grass and into the ground beneath it. Marlon walked towards it, his rifle at the ready. *Can never be too careful,* he thought. He put another bullet in the chamber to reload and slammed the bolt forward. He looked into its one remaining eye and saw that it was lifeless, just staring ahead. He heard a rustling, and again out of instinct pointed the rifle to his left. It was Larry, and he quickly put his hands up. His cheeks were wet with tears. "Jesus, Marlon! Put the gun down, it's just me! Did you get squashed? Are you hurt?" Marlon dropped the rifle behind him and moved up to hug Larry.

"Sorry, Lar, that brought me right back to the trenches. Yes, you old ninny, I'm fine. It would take more than a rogue buffalo to do me in." Larry smiled and disengaged from Marlon, he wiped his eyes with the palms of his hands.

"You scared me for a second is all. Ok, a few seconds. That was close Mar, too close for comfort. You are the finest shot that I have ever seen." Larry walked over to examine the buffalo, noticing the blood spilling out from around its eye.

"Hold on, his eye! Seriously Marlon I knew you were a great shot but how is that even possible? His eyes were half covered by fur and you hit it, while it was running, in the eye?"

Marlon stepped further from the riffle and closer to his lover. "I've been shooting for over thirty years and I guess I just got lucky. What can I tell you? Somehow when I really need to make a shot, I concentrate, pull the trigger, and I do it."

Larry dug through his pack, got out two cans and held up his index finger. "Yeah, fine, but that's Olympic skill level! I know you've been shooting for a long time but you don't train every day. Just bear with me, I'm going to run off and see how far away you can shoot and still be accurate."

Marlon scratched his head, but nodded and lay down on the ground. What's the harm? He got his rifle ready once more and waited for Larry to get back. Larry laid the tin cans down about five hundred feet away, about twenty feet apart, either would be a really hard shot in tall grass like this, even for Marlon.

Larry came back, huffing from jogging both times.

"M-make th-the f-first shot a-and, d-do the s-second blindfolded."

Marlon pushed his eyebrows together and turned his face up at him. "I can barely see the cans as it is. You're pulling my leg, right? Of course I can't do it blindfolded!"

Larry took a deep breath. "Just humor me. I've got a feeling about this."

Marlon shrugged his shoulders. *I've done crazier stuff, what the hell!* He looked into the scope, concentrated on the tiny reflection of light on the can and fired. A spilt second later there was a satisfying ting sound, just audible in the distance.

Larry whistled, "Woee! That's one hell of a shot! I think you got it. Now I'll point you in the right direction and blindfold you. Just concentrate like you told me you do and pull the trigger."

"Ok, Lar, I got lucky there but this is crazy. I've got no hope of hitting it blindfolded, but it's one bullet and I'll show you that I'm not magic or anything."

"You'll always be magical to me." Larry winked at him and passed him a handkerchief. Marlon smiled and took it, tying it around his head, adjusting it so he couldn't see. He felt Larry's strong hands on him, turning his shoulders and moving his gun. He adjusted his legs to be comfortable.

He laughed, "Silly Lar. I appreciate the confidence but c'mon. You really want me to do this?"

He felt Larry sit down beside him and heard a rustling sound. "Just give me a second to get out the binoculars. Yes, do it, please. I need to know."

Marlon ran his tongue along the inside of his teeth, trying to get something out between two of them. "Ok honey, for you I'll do it."

"I'm ready Mar, take the shot."

Marlon let out a deep breath. He concentrated on the target, his finger on the trigger. For a second he felt cold, like a cold mist around his feet but that was just his imagination. He concentrated again on where he thought the can could be and fired. For a spilt second, swirly white shapes appeared at the edges of his vision, just like those ones during the war on that terrible night. "Oh Jesus!" he jumped up and tore the blindfold off, stumbling and falling back down.

Larry was running forward and did not hear him. Marlon looked around but couldn't see any mist. The swirls were gone too. His chest heaved and he fought to catch his breath. With the sun shining and Larry holding up two cans and waving them about frantically, Marlon soon managed it. By the time Larry got back, he had forced a smile onto his face. By the time Larry got back, he had forced a smile. "Not a scratch on the second I know, you don't have to rub it in."

"No, two hits! I can hardly believe it myself, Mar, but look!"

Larry handed him the cans and there was no denying it. Both cans had holes through the middle of them. He didn't have a ruler but they might even have been in exactly the same spot on each. "This, this can't be. You're playing a trick right? You shot them yesterday when I wasn't around."

"No trick Mar, I'm as amazed as you are. I don't know what this means but it's some kind of miracle. You're touched by God. I can't explain it any other way."

I can't either, but God? I know magic exists and true evil exists, but anything else, well who knows?

Marlon took his hands, brought them up to his mouth and kissed each one. "Let's not talk about God. I'm a cold-hearted killer, Lar, God wouldn't bless me like that. You've never killed a man...shot him in the back as he ran off." Marlon suddenly felt ashamed. Then something caught the corner of his eye. He had been looking away from Larry, away from the dead buffalo and back towards the tree line. There was a figure with its head poking out from around a tree, like the buffalo, it was covered in brown shaggy fur. It was standing upright! Marlon distinctly heard it make a sort of surprised grunting sound as it noticed Marlon, and it ducked back into the woods.

Larry, not noticing, turned to face Marlon. "I know you had to do some terrible things in the war but everyone there did, you followed orders. God was on your side, not damming you. Besides, what else could you do? I didn't even have the courage to go, you'll always be a braver man than—"

Marlon held up his hand, "Shut up about that for second. Lar, did you see it? Look over at the tree line!" He pointed to where he had seen the creature, but only saw some trees rustling. "The tree branches are still moving, it was a sasquatch! C'mon, you're the expert tracker, let's get on its trail!"

Before Larry could even speak, Marlon had scooped up his rifle and had taken off at a dead run. "A sasquatch Mar, really? I think all the excitement with the shooting and the buffalo is playing tricks with you. Get back here!" he called out after him, but Marlon was already gone, he had always been the husky type while Marlon was lean and spry like a cat.

Larry jogged after him and saw that Marlon had already stopped. He had reached a spot ahead of Larry, and was scanning the ground. Larry put his hands on his knees to catch his breath. His words came in a rush between gasps, "Marlon-just-hold-on-a-minute, ok? Please don't-charge-off-by yourself. Could be-a bear around."

Marlon stopped and clapped his hands, then came over and helped Larry to stand. "I can look after myself Lar, I just saved my own hide, remember? Look what I found, I'm no tracking expert, but these look mighty peculiar to me." Larry looked down at what Marlon was trying to show him. On the ground, there was a big muddy spot but more importantly, there was a huge foot print in it. It was way bigger than any human-sized foot. Plus, the big toe was way off to the left, almost reminding him of some kind of chimpanzee, but he knew that that was impossible out here in the woods.

"Marlon, I'll give it to you that that is the weirdest damned track that I ever did see. Whatever it was, it even has webbed toes. I'd say from the size of the print that he'd also have to be at least eight feet tall, and four hundred pounds, maybe more. But let's just hold it. Bears have been known to walk on two legs, maybe this one is injured, got his paw stuck in a trap or—"

Marlon held up a finger, "No dammit, it's a creature. I saw him and I know what a bear looks like. This thing had a human-like face! It will be the picture of the century! Think of the money we'll get for it! C'mon, before it gets too far ahead." Larry grabbed Marlon by the arm and held him tight.

"A sasquatch, Mar? Come on, you know better than that. There are a lot of things out in the woods, but the missing link ain't one of 'em. No, let's go back and skin the buffalo, that'll take a while, and we can head back to the cabin. We won't make it back before sunset as it is."

Marlon wrenched free of his grip and moved his arms to get the backpack from his shoulders. "Yes,

Lar, I do know better. And fuck the buffalo! I didn't want to show you this, but I'm not the tracker you are, and I need your help. I saw things in France, things that would turn your shit white! You don't need to believe me, I have proof." Marlon dug out an old leather-bound book with a clasp at the front. He unclasped it and brought out four pictures.

"You're starting to scare me, Mar. War does strange things to a man. I saw it tear apart my own Pa. He was a mean son-of-a-bitch after the Great War. Drank like a fish, and wouldn't hesitate to give me and Ma a good whippin', but that still don't mean that fairy tales come true. It's just that trauma messes with you. Still though, if it makes you feel better, show them to me. I've seen a dead body before—found my Pa with his head blown off—this can't be any worse than that."

Marlon's face lost all expression as he handed him the photos, "Don't say I didn't warn you. This is worse than a corpse, this one wouldn't stay down."

Larry studied the pictures, his eyes opening wide and his fingers starting to quiver. The first one showed a field of soldiers, their uniforms in tatters. They all had rotten flesh that hung from their faces and hands. One had an eyeball out of its socket on his cheek, another had no nose, but they all stood rigid at attention in a forest, all with their rifles held in front of them. Some of the hands were skeletal, others were black and putrid looking. It was an action sequence as a man with blond hair, all disheveled looking, swung the butt of his rifle at one of the dead men. In the second photo, the thing was half to the ground. In the third, it was on the ground, and in the fourth, it was back up. You could see that whoever took the picture got closer each time, to make sure there could be no mistake of what happened in the grizzly scene.

Larry understood the full horror of the situation, he flicked the photos away in disgust, his face twisted into an ugly sneer, and he turned to one side to vomit. Falling to his knees in disbelief, Marlon was behind him and rubbed his back. "I'm sorry, Larry, but I had to show you. You had to know the truth. You always asked, and now it's done. The war did change me but not just from the killing. In the war I saw that magic was real, pure evil walked the earth, and me and the boys had to put it back down. Now, that thing in the woods is out there. I know it, and now you know it. Maybe it ain't evil, maybe it's just scared, but whatever the hell it is we have to find it. We have to do our best. I couldn't live with myself if I didn't."

Larry wiped his mouth and though shaking, managed to stand up. "I...that was...don't ever show me those again. Please put them away, Marlon. I can't deny what I saw, you fought some fucking Satan-worshipper, or Nazi cultist or something in France; someone made those abominations. I'll help you track it and we'll see what it does, but you have to promise me that this is the end. A sasquatch isn't some demon, even if it's real. Christ you got me talking about some mythical creature like it exists. Everything I ever heard about them just says they are the missing link, a freak of nature. I love you and I'll always be here for you, but this...this isn't natural, and I can't be a part of it. We find this and hopefully make a fortune with this picture but then it's done. We'll lead a normal life, as normal as we can, and I'll help you forget about whatever happened in France. I'll get you pills, take you to doctors, whatever it takes, but it all ends with this hunt."

He doesn't get it, Marlon thought. *It will never end for me. Evil has touched my soul and once it's there, it will find me wherever I go and whatever I do. I know that this sasquatch thing is hopefully just a weird animal but I can't be certain until I see it. I have to try and set the world right again somehow, with or without Larry. This creature may be tainted; maybe there is someone in a cabin making it do things, making it evil. Garry's letter convinced me that evil is out there, and if the boys keep destroying it then I have to as well.* He extended his hand, looked Larry deep in the eyes and told him, "It's a deal, Lar, I swear it. I'll put it all behind me. Now let's get behind this thing, it's already got one hell of a head start on us."

Larry nodded, adjusted the pack on his shoulders and put his head down. Watching for tracks, he motioned with his arm overhead for Marlon to follow. Marlon picked up the pictures from the ground, tucked them back inside his book, and got his camera out. He wound it up and took a picture of the biggest footprint he had ever seen.

☐

Footprints Part 2

Marlon followed his boyfriend, Larry, into the woods outside of Juneau, Alaska. It was mid-June and the weather had finally warmed up as of late. That still meant wearing long pants and a light jacket, but that didn't matter right now. *The missing link*, Marlon thought, *Larry would never believe it, but after what I saw in the war I know that what I saw was real. The world is full of wonderful and terrible things, and this one isn't about to get away.* Larry was tall, over six feet, and stocky, weighing a good two-twenty. He was muscled, but was working on a beer belly. Marlon don't mind. He liked someone with some meat on his bones and some hair to keep him warm at night. Marlon was slimmer, about five-ten and under one-eighty. He liked to exercise and enjoyed hiking, climbing, and swimming, though here he could only get in the water three or four months of the year, with the last month and the first always being on the chilly side.

Larry walked with his head down, following the tracks. Marlon kept his rifle in-hand and scanned the area. He wanted a picture of the creature, but knew it could be hostile. Hell, he had almost been killed by a buffalo earlier that morning, so he was looking out for both their skins. He made sure the rifle was loaded and turned around to look behind them for a second. The woods had gotten thicker, the sunshine now making thin slivers form all around them in the mid-morning light. The normal sounds of woodpeckers, squirrels, and birds were in his ears, along with the scraping and rustling sounds Larry and he made as they pushed past a tree branch or scraped through a tall bush. Larry had shown him a few things about tracking, and while he could identify a few animals by their prints, Marlon was useless at the actual tracking part. *So hard to walk in the forest and constantly keep looking down*, he thought, *Larry must still have the trail though, or he would have said something.* Sweat had begun to bead on his forehead. He called out, "Hold up Lar, need to wet my whistle." Larry raised his right hand and stopped. He began to dig through his pack.

Marlon opened up his own knapsack and found his canteen. He took a long draught, put the cap back on, and replaced it in the pack.

"Still got the trail Mar, whatever this is, it is moving and its strides are long. We'll have to hope it tires before us and just goes back to its lair. Remember, I need you to be my spotter, let me know if you see anything threatening, or a big hole or something ahead of me."

Marlon nodded, "Of course hon, I got your hairy back. Keep moving, it's almost noon already." Larry chuckled, turned his head and winked at him, then continued to hike. Larry would stop occasionally and make marks on the trees. He would carve an *X* with his knife or he would fish out some chalk from his pocket and draw an arrow pointing back. *Smart*, Marlon thought, *I would have been lost by now for sure*. The ground was uneven and Marlon found he couldn't always look up. There were roots and tree stumps, some dead fallen trees and the occasional hole, small though, maybe made by gophers or hedgehogs.

They continued their journey and the woods began to thin a little, Marlon noticed that some of the trees were blackened, and there were even more stumps and small trees. *Regrowth*, he thought. *Must have been a fire here, maybe a year or so ago. Nature always finds a way to come back.* His thoughts were interrupted as he heard his stomach rumble. *Must be lunch time.* Looking around, he saw that the blackened area was not a bad place to stop. "How about we stop here, Lar? I could go for a bite."

Larry nodded and dropped his pack to the ground, quickly slumping down to sit on a stump. He took out his water and had a long drink, wiping his mouth with the back of his hand. He dug out a sandwich wrapped in wax paper and Marlon did the same. He walked over to sit on the stump beside him. "Do you think we're gaining on him?" he said in between bites. The caribou meat was heavily salted, but the mustard on it was pleasant enough. *Beggars can't be choosers. At least breakfast at Joe's Cafe was usually good.*

Larry wiped the sweat from his face with the back of his hand and laid his sandwich in his lap. "Pass me your water, love, I'm getting low." Marlon did as he was asked and Larry had a small swig of it. "Thanks, I haven't heard him yet, but that doesn't mean much. The creature could be good at moving through the woods, and a lot quieter than us I'd say. You're good in open fields, but these thick woods are a bugger."

Marlon nodded, starting to work on the other half of his sandwich. "Yeah, that adds up." Larry gave him a long look and Marlon stopped eating. "Ok, Lar, I know that look, what's up?"

"What's up? Seriously? You showed me pictures of zombies in uniforms standing at attention with rifles. You think that hasn't been rolling around in my head all morning? I don't know if I'll ever sleep again. I need to know more Mar, what happened? How did you beat those...monsters?"

Marlon coughed and felt his airway close up. Reaching for the canteen, he took a swig of water and coughed. "Almost made me choke, Lar! Yeah, I should have known you'd say that. For me it was years ago, but I agree it's a lot to take in. I suppose you won't go any further unless I tell you?"

Larry continued munching, swallowed and nodded. "You got it pal, I ain't taking another step further until you fess up. We promised we wouldn't keep secrets from each other. I'm scared but also mad as hell at you. You owe me the truth."

Marlon's shoulders slumped and he let out a long sigh. He finished off the last square of his sandwich and ran his fingers through his hair. "Ok, Lar, I'm sorry I didn't tell you this before. I just wasn't sure how you would take it. You know what the war did to me. I was trying to spare you some of that. I told you all about the Battle of the Bulge, we don't need to get into it again. I was already shell-shocked from that, but I guess it hadn't set in yet. The next day we were given a weird mission by our CO. Some fool, a Lieutenant Dodd, had managed to get himself and his whole company lost in Longvilly, Belgium, not far from where we were. I was already confused; why send two more battalions after one lost one? Soon, I found out that Dodd's father was a general, and he wouldn't rest until the boy was found. The general assigned us a French tracker, Louis was his name I think, along with some other specialists, and even a civilian. It was a fella by the name of Dr. Angel. He was some kind of expert in the occult, and I guess I should have known then that that was going to be no ordinary mission. I had been exhausted though, and the general told us all that if we found Dodd, we would get a ticket home the next day. Everyone wanted out of that frozen hell-hole, and we set out at first rise on the morning of January 1st, 1945."

Larry was a slower eater, and chewed on his sandwich. Laying his pack down, he took off his boots and socks. Marlon held his nose and waved. Larry laughed and said, "You can handle it, soldier boy. Keep going, it's just the two of us."

Saying that made Marlon think of being snuck up on and he glanced around nervously. He continued his story. "So that first day was fine, it was cold enough to freeze the balls off a brass monkey, but we were used to that. We looked through the woods; Louis looked for traps, Dr. Angel checked his books and mumbled to himself mostly, and the rest of the crew just bided their time. I tried to stay alert, the front wasn't too far off and there could have been Nazis anywhere. Turns out I was right.

That night a cold mist came up all around us and the gunnery sergeant, Wilson, I think, went down in a heap with a bullet between his eyes. Luckily, it hadn't been a sniper, or he could have taken down a lot of us. I had been on watch, but I'll admit that the days and the weeks had worn me down, and I had been napping. When I woke up, despite all the shouting and the shooting, I first felt the mist. It seemed to emanate from the ground and it didn't just feel cold, it felt unnatural. As if it was sucking the life out of me, my feet went numb all of sudden.

Of course we were all awake then and the Germans charged us. I don't know how they could have even seen us through the mist. In an instant it was all around us, right up in our faces, it was. I'll tell you, Lar, it was bad. While the fighting started with guns, it soon became hand-to-hand. I ended up rolling into a trench that I hadn't even known was there. I had this young German with his hands wrapped around my throat, and I nearly passed out. The fall knocked him off me and I managed to get my knife out. I was so mad that I must have stabbed him twenty times. I just kept cutting until there was almost nothing left of his face, poor son of a bitch. He hadn't even looked old enough to shave." Larry came over and held him tight and patted his back. When he pulled away, he began to retie his boots.

"Sounds like hell, all right. Continue, Mar, I know at least some of you must have made it out of the scrap. We better get movin' though if we want to catch this thing."

Marlon nodded. Standing up, they both continued into the forest. "Thanks, Lar. Yeah it was the most up-close and personal I got with the Jerries, and even though we won, things weren't good. Another two people were dead, and a private fell down into some hidden part of a bunker and broke his arm. We had to go down there after him and that's when things got real weird. This hidden room mostly just held ammo and rations. The professor, who somehow didn't have a scratch on him, found this book. It looked like it was bound in dark leather. I wasn't sure, but somehow the cover looked like a face, and I made a point then not to look at it or at the prof whenever possible. The CO, Smythe, was eagle-eyed and found a loose board in the wall.

When he took it out, there was a ladder leading down."

Larry stretched his neck from side to side. Marlon smiled, "You set?" Larry nodded.

"Anyway, our commanding officer, Lieutenant Smythe, was a stickler and ordered us forward. 'Dodd could be anywhere, even down this tunnel.' A few of us grumbled and I thought it was nuts, but he repeated the order and started to climb down. We all moved forward and descended into the tunnel. Let me tell you the place reeked, not just of dead rats and shit, but of death. Some of the men puked. I breathed through my mouth and we pressed on. Soon enough things went completely bonkers. We entered into this big chamber, and there were a good twenty men there along with Dodd. He was on top of some kind of altar and they had him in a chair made out of bones. They had symbols carved in his chest, arms, and legs. Some of them I knew; the swastika, a pentagram, an ankh, but the others I had no clue about. I don't know how the poor soul wasn't screaming, but his eyes were open, just staring ahead. The man doing the cutting was wearing a red robe, and the others were in black ones. All of them had swastika arm bands. The cultists were all chanting while the guy in the red robe seemed to be speaking a weird guttural language, making his voice rise and fall as he completed a symbol on Dodd."

Larry interrupted, his hands fell from his face and he almost tripped over a tree root. "Sweet Jesus! No wonder you have nightmares. I know the Nazis were evil pieces of shit, but cultists, and a book made out of human skin?" Marlon gave him a stern look, narrowing his eyebrows together.

"This is not an easy story to tell, you wanted to hear it so just listen, alright?" Larry reached forward and held his hand for a second.

"Sorry Mar, it's just so unbelievable, please continue."

Marlon took a sip of water and went on. "The worst part is coming. Some of the men just fainted, others puked, another ran away, and Smythe just froze. So a corporal took control, and told us to open fire but to avoid hitting Dodd. I didn't need any encouragement. I took my time and aimed right for the head cultist, but at the last second these swirly white shapes appeared in the air. It made me blink and I missed by just a hair. I blew the bastard's ear off and the chanting stopped, but the whole gang was on us then. We had one guy with a flamethrower, and another with grenades. The Nazis had guns but they never stood a chance. We mowed them down like weeds. The main guy drew a knife and charged me. This time I didn't miss, got him right in the throat and he went down. As soon as I got the red-robed guy, the swirly white shapes faded away, not that it was really any better. Two of the Nazis were ablaze and the grenades had taken out five more. Some of the men were fighting hand-to-hand with cultists while others were in a gun battle. If you never live to see men run around on fire and screaming, you're a lucky man. That was a horrendous sight and I'll admit that I froze, and a few seconds later I tossed my cookies."

A ray of sunshine fell on Larry's face and Marlon couldn't mistake his look, eyes wide, mouth slack, a combination of horror and fascination. *At least he hadn't been there*, he thought, *telling it doesn't even capture half of the horror.* "When I came back to my senses it was all over except for the screaming. Two more of our men were dead, and all the Nazis were either dead or badly wounded. Incredibly, Dodd was still sitting there in the chair, just staring ahead. The men finished off the Nazis. I know they should have been prisoners, but as I said, no one was acting normal anymore. I went up and cut the bonds on Dodd. He felt like a sack of potatoes and never said a word, but I managed to drag him down from the stage. Smythe finally had snapped out of it and ordered us out of there. The roof had started to come down in flakes and chips, so he didn't have to tell me twice. The professor, who had a bullet in his arm and a bad cut across his face, ran up on the head cultist and rifled through his robes, taking the dagger he had used and whatever else was on him. Somehow we got out of there and made it back to the surface."

Larry reached over and took a hold of Marlon's hands, he hadn't noticed how bad they were shaking. "I have to interrupt. Thank you for sharing this with me. It's like some kind of terrible movie or pulp fiction, but I know if you're telling it, then it happened. Jesus, did you get Dodd back to his father?"

Marlon griped Larry's hands tight in his. The shaking subsided and he let go of one, reaching up to wipe away a tear from his eye with two fingers. "Thank you, Lar. Somehow it does feel better to share, to get it off my chest. My friend Gary knows about this, he was there. It's why I didn't show you his letters. I wanted to spare you from what ha—" Marlon stopped in mid-sentence. Mist had started to form around his feet and he jumped, he could feel the coldness spreading into his toes. "Jesus Lar, do you see that? Look at the ground!"

Larry was moving slowly, drawing an arrow with a piece of chalk, he stopped and looked down. "So it's some fog rolling in? Not that strange, temperature is just dropping a little."

Marlon's eyes opened wide, his heart immediately started to pound, sounding like a jackhammer in his ears. *Can't let it get Larry, have to get out of here!* He reached to grab Larry, almost wrenching his arm from the socket.

"Move, God damn you! I don't know the way out, we have to leave, you heard about the mist in France, move!" He had never used that tone with

Larry, had never given him an order like he had heard his commanding officer do, but he couldn't risk it, already his feet were starting to go numb.

Larry blinked, his mouth opened a little and his eyebrows furrowed together. "Ouch! You really yanked me hard that time! You know my feet do feel cold all of sudden. Yeah I...I don't like this either. Watch for the marks I made in the trees, big cuts making an x and white chalk marks pointing out, I'll try to keep up."

"I'm not leaving you behind; no man gets left behind. Get moving!" Marlon screamed the last part at the top of his lungs and they bolted forward. It wasn't easy with all the roots and holes in the ground. Larry fell once, as did Marlon, painfully twisting his ankle so that Larry had to help him. But they moved on, spotting one mark on a tree and chalk on another. The mist had started to rise. It was at their ankles now.

"Mar, I can't feel my feet, it feels as if I'm running on blocks of ice. Fuck me, you're right! We need to get out!" Marlon looked about frantically. The trees were still thick. He couldn't see the tall grass from where they had started this morning. Everything felt tight; his chest felt like it was going to explode, and his heart felt like it would leap out through his throat at any second. The trees seems to be closing in on them, he felt like he was back in France, just waiting for the first bullet to split the air.

Marlon looked down for a second. *Legs are numb up to my knees but somehow I'm moving. I don't feel the pain in my ankle.* "Your feet are there, Lar, just keep moving! We'll get out. You are the best woodsman I've ever seen. I know you can do it." Larry nodded and Marlon was glad to see a small smile creep onto one side of his face. He pointed with his right arm to a mark, an arrow pointing to the east, the way they were going. *You better be*, he thought, *I'll be damned if I die in a forest, killed by some fucking mist. I made it out of the war; I'll make it out of here!*

Time passed, the mist swirled about their legs. Sounds grew twisted, the birds sounded like they were underwater. Marlon thought that he heard growling from somewhere behind him, and in another second, he thought he heard something whiz by his nose. But when he reached up and felt his nose, there was no blood on his hand. The shapes started to form, the same swirls he had seen in the cultist's chambers. They were translucent for now but he didn't know how long that would last.

He didn't know if the chanting he heard in his ears was real, or if he was just reliving that terrible day, that time when the real face of the enemy had been shown to him somewhere beneath Longvilly. Both of his legs were now numb, and he saw from the look on Larry's face that he was not doing well. The veins pulsed in his neck and his face was as red as a beet. *We better get out of here soon, I don't know how much more either of us can take. The swirly shapes are beginning to look like the yin and yang symbol, only all white,* Marlon thought, *and there are more of them now, at least a dozen following us.*

The symbols were all around them now, maybe fifty of them. Marlon had to squint to see through them. The sun seemed to have almost disappeared, and Marlon felt the numbness spread into his stomach and creep up to his chest. "Larry, I want you to know that I loved you right from the start." He could barely get the words out, he was desperately out of breath and his lungs didn't seem to be working right. He didn't know how Larry was still on his feet.

Larry looked at him, looked deep into his eyes and said, "I know Mar, I did too." Then he turned ahead and said, "The light! Christ on a cracker, we made it!" Larry and Marlon collapsed past the tree line in a heap and lay in the late afternoon sun. The mist seemed to recoil. Tendrils that almost looked like fingers seemed to scratch at them and were then slowly pulled back into the deep woods. Marlon looked up and saw the buffalo lying dead a short distance away. Flies were buzzing around it, and he could smell the rotting flesh from here. Most of his body had that prickly, tingling sensation like when one's foot falls asleep. He let out a small laugh and started to cry, "Sweet Jesus Lar, you did it, you got us out. I...I'll never be able to thank you enough. I'll tell you everything, but not here. We've still got a good four hours before it gets dark. Let's spend a night in town, ok? I need to be around as many lights and people as possible, just for tonight."

Larry held Marlon tight and stroked his hair. "I am an expert woodsman after all, you said so yourself. Get your scrawny ass up. Yeah, I agree, the cabin can wait until tomorrow. Besides, that buffalo is only worm food now." Marlon wiped away his tears and they both limped off together. His foot had painfully come back to life and he knew that he would certainly have a badly swollen ankle for a few days. Something made him turn back, the swirly shapes around the forest were all dissipating, being burned away by the sunlight, but he could have sworn that the last one was in the shape of a swastika. A horrible, twisted laugh seemed to fill his ears, only to also fade away with the crunching of a twig beneath his feet.

☐

It's a Small World

The water in front of Mark was so clear and so shallow. He closed his eyes for a second and breathed in the warm air. No smell of exhaust or garbage, just the clean ocean air. The water was green and he could see the white sand just a few feet beneath him. He looked to the side and his wife, Natalie, was walking on the bottom. She had black sunglasses on and her blonde hair was wet and lay on the back of her neck. It looked darker than usual with the water in it. *I love this place*, he thought, *so quiet, warm, and peaceful. On this whole beach we're the only people here, well us and that pelican.* He looked up and saw the pelican sitting on top of a wooden pole a hundred feet or so ahead of him. They were in Green Turtle Cay, a small island in the Bahamas about a forty minute boat ride from Marsh Harbour Airport. Mark had been coming here since he had been a child, and he especially loved that the place had barely changed in thirty years. He was also glad that his parents had been able to come along with them. His dad had cancer, and he wanted to go everywhere he could with his father while he was still in remission.

The island only had about four hundred people on it and certainly didn't have much in terms of attractions, but Mark didn't mind. As long as he was somewhere warm and could get outside to walk and swim he was happy. It was a pleasant seventy-five out and the water was keeping him cool. After the swim, he was looking forward to going back to Round Pound House—the place they had rented—having a drink, and reading some comics. He continued to swim out towards the pole. The water was so shallow that they could be further from the shore than normal. Mark figured that they were a good eight or nine hundred feet out. The beach was in a protected cove, and there were no waves, nor undercurrents. Mark knew that they were safe. He looked towards the pelican sitting on top of the wooden poll just ahead of him. Smiling to himself, he thought, *the pelican is a funny bird, his bill can hold more than his belly can*. That was a fact that his father-in-law often said. Looking to Natalie, he saw a plastic tube sticking out of the water where her head had been. *Snorkeling again. I could never get into it; I always found it annoying to keep blowing water out of the tube.*

Looking up again, he saw the pelican. It had brown fuzzy feathers on the top of its head, orange skin around its eyes that went down into its beak, and black feathers on its wings and back. It had a long neck, a long bill, and of course the huge pouch beneath. *Really strange looking birds; much different from those back in Newfoundland.* Mark knew this one was searching for fish, but right now it was looking at him. He swam closer, wondering how near he could get to the pole before it would fly off. The water was warm and the sun beat down on him. The heat under his black hat made him feel glad that he was wearing sunglasses and sunscreen. Putting his feet down, he felt the soft squish of sand beneath his toes. It was so nice to be out this far and touch bottom. He heard a gentle splash and walked towards the pole. Natalie poked her head out of the water, took her mask off, and pushed her hair back out of her face. "Watch out for that pelican!" she called out, "He may not like you getting too close."

"Don't be silly," he replied, "I'm not going to try and climb the pole, he doesn't care about me." He was close now, maybe ten feet. The bird's gaze was unwavering, and it remained perfectly still and stared at him. It was almost like a feathered, freakish statue, at least until it blinked. Mark was starting to feel a little nervous; it was a big bird and he had never been this close to one before. Turing his head, he saw his wife continue to swim closer. She would be there in a minute.

Determined not to let fear stop him, he swam the last few feet and reached out to touch the pool. The bird turned its head ever so slightly, just enough to look right down at him. Their eyes meet for a split second and he thought he saw annoyance, maybe even anger in them, but he knew that it was just his imagination. His wife called out, "That's close enough. Stop bothering the pelican, please." He nodded and walked away. Moving towards her, he noticed that she seemed a little pale. Her hand had moved to her stomach.

"Are you feeling ok?"

She shook her head, "I may have eaten too much junk today. You know, that and all the booze we've had this trip can upset my stomach."

Mark frowned, "Well, it's probably time to head back to shore. Lie down for a while before we go back?"

Their towels, beach bag, and sandals were just as they had left them. Mark saw movement in his periphery vision and turned his head. Another couple strolled onto the beach. He couldn't tell much about them from this distance other than that they were white tourists just like he and Natalie. He plumped down on the towel, fished out a bottle of water from the bag, and started to drink. He motioned with the bottle to Natalie, and she took it from him and had a swig. Mark began to get all of the sand off his feet. He hated that coarse, grimy feeling on them, and cleaned them carefully.

He looked to the side again, curious, and saw the couple further down the beach taking off their shirts and lying down on their stomachs to tan. The woman was topless but that wasn't strange; the beach was almost deserted and he had seen it done before at a hotel in Key West, and on a beach in the Dominican Republic. *She isn't shy*, he thought, and went back to work on his feet. He heard Natalie clear her throat and make a long sigh. He turned to her and noticed that her eyebrows were pushed together, her lips pressed tight.

"Something wrong? Is your stomach still bad? I can stop cleaning my feet and we can go back."

She shook her head, her eyes looked full, like tears were about to spill over her lashes. "I actually had to go outside to puke in the grass early this morning."

Mark stopped what he was doing and sat up straight. His heart had started to pound hard in his chest. His throat felt like it would close over. "Are you saying that you had morning sickness? You remember that I had a vasectomy about six weeks ago." He took a deep breath. *After five years of marriage and ten years of being together, is it possible that she cheated on me? I've never cheated, sure maybe I considered it idly a couple of times, but I never would have done it. They were just fantasies.* He felt his own eyes start to fill up.

She reached out and took his hand. He knew this was serious; Natalie hadn't held hands with him in years; she didn't like it. "No, it's too early for morning sickness. But look, you know I'd never cheat on you. I know you must think that I couldn't get pregnant, but you're wrong. I looked online and it says that a man can still have active sperm for two months afterwards. It's been less time than that I'm afraid. I took a test and it was positive. I'll take another if you want."

The full horror of her statement set in. His heart was pounding a mile a minute, his vision began to blur, and tiny spirals appeared at the edges of his vision. Terror like he had never felt before slid their icy fingers around his mind, his heart, and his lungs. He had never wanted responsibility; he had never wanted a management position. Hell, he had even put off marriage until he was thirty, and now he would be responsible to look after his own flesh and blood, a lifelong responsibility that would never really go away.

"I might pass out, I need to lie back." He lay back on the towel, Natalie reclined back as well, still holding his hand. "I checked on that too," her voice was a whisper, "I know the way your mind works. Pregnancy tests are ninety-nine percent accurate." Tears had spilled out and begun to run down her cheeks.

His mind began to churn, desperate to come up with a solution. *I never wanted kids; that's why I got fixed. Ninety-nine isn't for certain, there's a small chance. We could give it up for adoption or even have an abortion. My life will be over; no more free time, no seeing my friends, no poker, no trips.* Once more she seemed to read his thoughts, and she let his hand go. She dug in her pocket for a tissue, wiped her eyes, and spoke. Mark blinked back tears. He reached up and began to pull at his beard, a nervous habit he had developed over the past few years. "I know it's a long shot, but you'll have to get a blood test when we get back home to be certain. You don't seem to be showing yet, so we don't need to mention it to Mom and Dad."

Natalie nodded, "Yes, I will. You need to face reality though, almost certainly I'm pregnant and we have a lot of decisions to make. The chances of me getting pregnant at thirty-nine and with you being snipped, well it's like winning the lotto. We were meant to have this baby, I won't accept anything else." Her voice was stronger now, her eyes piercing as they looked into his. "I'll leave you if you try to make me get rid of it, don't think I won't do it." Mark sat up and put his head in his hands, wiping away a few stray tears. The waves made a gentle lapping noise against the sand, though it was just barely heard over his pounding heart. "You don't need to make threats. I never wanted kids, but I know how you feel. If you really are pregnant we'll figure it out, my life as I know it will be over, but I don't have a choice. I'll just have to become an older dad like my friends did, just hopefully not divorced like them." He smiled a little and looked up. Natalie's eyes were red but she smiled too. She came over and hugged him tight, whispering in his ear.

"It won't be the end of your life, just different for a few years. We'll get help like your brother does and we'll make it work. I would like to head back to the house though, and I'm sure you could use a drink."

Sure as hell I could, he thought, *I have always felt that I can figure out any problem in my life, I just need enough time. In this case nine months will have to do it*. He put on his sandals and put the blanket away. Wiping his eyes once more and getting out the water bottle, he twisted off the cap and took a long draught of water. His throat felt dry and raw, and the water helped some. He cleared his throat and Natalie put her towel in the bag and they started to walk towards the other couple. The woman had rolled over and her breasts were in full view. Mark leaned over to his wife and whispered, "If you are pregnant, your boobs will get bigger, and that will be fun for me."

She punched him playfully in the shoulder and whispered, "Horny devil! They won't get like hers though. They are huge, could be fake. What do you think?"

Mark couldn't help but look now. They were big but lolled to the sides a little like Natalie's did. He had seen porn and obviously fake breasts, but never in person. These were real as far as he knew. The woman, who certainly had a nice figure Mark had noticed, grew ever closer. Natalie elbowed him and whispered, "Don't stare, it's rude!" Mark consciously looked away, his face felt red with embarrassment.

He felt it best to change the topic, "So you do want to go out to dinner tonight? We haven't been to that Lizard Bar place. That is if your stomach has settled down."

Natalie looked ahead, perhaps also made uncomfortable by the public nudity. "Yes, sure we can do that, my stomach should be ok. I'll get some toast and maybe a little rice for a snack."

The woman opened her eyes and sat up just before they passed by. "Excuse me, I couldn't help but notice your accents. Are you from Newfoundland?"

Mark found himself staring at her breasts again. *I just can't help it*, he thought, *they are right in front of me*. He held the beach bag in front of his stomach to hide his excitement. The man next to her rolled over and sat up.

Natalie replied, "Oh, um, yes we are. I'm from St. John's, and my husband is from CBS, which is just outside it."

The woman smiled and clapped her hands together. Her breasts barely moved. They certainly did seem more like balls than normal fatty tissue. "I knew it! I'm from Nova Scotia but my husband here is from Stephenville." The husband stood up and extended his hand. Mark was glad to be able to focus on him, and shook his hand.

"I'm Doug, funny isn't it? All the way down 'ere in the Bahamas and we meet some Newfies. What are the odds?"

The guy had a firm grip. "Nice to meet you Doug, I'm Mark, and this is my wife, Natalie." The woman stood up and shook Natalie's hand. "Oh, and I'm Justine. We might go to that Lizard place you mentioned too, it's down that road going to the Marina right?"

Natalie nodded. "Yeah that's right, it's on the left and there are some houses on the side of it, you can't miss it. The sign has a lizard painted on it. I have to say you have a lovely figure."

Justine smiled back, "How sweet are you! Thank you, your hair is lovely. Well, we don't want to bother you, I'm white as a ghost and would like to work on my tan."

Dough clapped Mark on the shoulders, "Nice to meet you, me son. It's a small world ain't it? Well, enjoy yer holiday."

Mark smiled, "No bother, nice to meet the both of you." They smiled and waved as Mark and Natalie walked on. Natalie waved back. Once they were out of earshot she said, "Well that took your mind of the news for bit. I'd like to have a shower when we get back. Is six ok with you to leave?"

Mark nodded, "Yeah, six is fine. I see it now, fake boobs might look ok but I bet they feel weird." It's a small world after all, Mark thought back to a few years ago when they had been at Disney World. For old time's sake they had gone to the Magic Kingdom, had done all the old rides, and incredibly, had also met a Newfoundlander there too. Her name had been Linda, and she had been a teacher that he used to work with. The sun beat down on his face. He fished his hat out of the bag and put it on, followed by his shades. *I guess the next time I'll be in Disney, I'll have a kid. It's a small world for sure and mine's about to get a lot more full.*

"It's a small world after all, it's a small world after all, it's a small world after all, it's a small, small world." The song escaped from his lips in a whisper as they moved up from the beach, entered the tree line, and headed up the trail to the rental house.

Another Day in Paradise

Mike squinted against the setting sun. Despite his clip on shades, he found it a little difficult to see as the sun hung low in the sky almost directly at eye level. He was driving on the right hand side of the car and on the left hand side of the road, a strange thing for anyone from Canada. The water was close, too close to the side of the road. Driving on the left hand side was so foreign to him, but luckily there was sticker on the windshield with an arrow pointing left. The road was small, just barely big enough for two cars, and with all the potholes he had to slow down even more, until he was just crawling along. The ocean to this left was the Caribbean Ocean. He had learned that from a plaque next to the narrow bridge they had been on earlier. The ocean was a beautiful shade of greenish blue, so clear and bright, so different from the dark waters of the Atlantic back home in Newfoundland. The van was old, he had looked in the glove compartment yesterday and had seen that it was a 2003. *Fourteen years old*, he thought, *that was the best they could give me. Not much value for over four hundred bucks. In the States, I could have gotten a brand new car for fifty bucks a day. Here for over a hundred you get an old piece of crap*. The air conditioning worked as did everything important, but it shook, rattled, and bumped up and down. He couldn't get it much past seventy clicks an hour; above that it vibrated so much that he thought it might go off the road. He reached down and took up the water bottle from the center console. Squeezing it, he had a drink and laid it back down.

His wife and dad were in the back, and his mom was seated in the front. "Turn on some air back here!" his dad called out. They were on the island of Eleuthera. They had spent the whole day driving around to get to this marina. He had had to ask directions six times, had taken at least six wrong turns, and had had to listen to his parents argue about which direction was the right way for what felt like hours. *Why didn't I get a roaming package on my cell? Google Maps would have made today so much simpler.* It had taken three hours to find the Marina and once they had gotten there, he had only been able to have one drink with lunch, and had spent the whole time trying to keep flies away from his food. *All these outdoor restaurants are great in theory but with so many flies around, they're not so good in practice.* His mom had her hand twisted around the seatbelt. "You know it's weird, my pants are smaller all of sudden?"

Mike smiled. She could say the funniest things sometimes.

"Maybe the racoon did it; came in and switched out your pants one night." His dad spoke up from the back, "Or it could have been the homeless guy who took your tomatoes!" Mike was laughing, everyone in the car was. That was a good one. That tomato plant she had planted in Florida last year had grown a few green tomatoes on it one day, and the next day they had been gone. His mom had come to the crazy conclusion that it had been a homeless person, when clearly it had been a racoon. He had seen one around the house in Grant, and they were clever bastards, or so his friend Jim had told him. The laughing took away the tiredness he felt in his mind and body for a few seconds and he announced, "I'm going to turn into the Shell station just down the road, we are getting low on gas." *The Bahamas, well at least this island, is just not doing well. They don't produce anything here, and shipping it all in must be pricey. I suppose I should be used to it. On every island I've been to it's been the same; gas is really expensive, food, and lodgings. Alcohol seems to be one of the only cheap things to be found.*

There was construction up ahead on Haynes Avenue, so he tried to turn on his signal to go right. He turned on the windshield wiper by mistake again. *So hard to get used to,* he thought, *the windshield wiper on the right, and turn signal on the left. There are so many opposites in this car. And how come the street signs are in miles per hour but the van's speedometer is in kilometers? Wacky!* He looked off into the horizon for a second. After the gas, *I'll stop by that gambling place, Lucky's. Maybe they will have poker and I can head back there later to play.* Music drifted through the van and he recognized the voice of Phil Collins.

Oh, think twice, it's another day for you and me in paradise.

He started to make the turn to go right into the gas station, the windshield wiper flicked on. Mike's moment of distraction meant that he didn't look to see if there was a car in the other lane.

His eyes opened wide, *there is a car coming towards us, fuck!* He told his hands to turn the wheel but it was too late, his mom called out in a breaking, almost crying voice, "We're gonna hit!" The van slammed into the front of the other car. It was silver in color and some kind of Honda. The impact hit the Honda on the driver's side and caused both of the vehicles to be pushed backwards. Mike had been on roller coasters, and he had done bumper cars. Hell, he had been in an accident where his jeep had been airborne and had ended up on its side, but he had never felt an impact like this. The airbags saved him from smashing his face against the wheel. Instead, it was his chest that felt the impact. Fortunately the adrenaline was pumping and his chest muscles felt just a dull ache for the moment.

Immediately he said, "Is everyone ok?" there were replies in the affirmative and his parents and wife got out of the car. There was smoke coming from in front of him and he was trying to get the key out but it was stuck. There was a loud ringing in his left ear. His mind told him that it was tinnitus, a temporary condition caused from a loud noise that he had experienced before. It made the people talking and the noises around him muffled, like it was all under water.

"Mike!" it was his wife, Nicole's, voice, "Get out of the car!" He responded slowly, finally checking to make sure that he wasn't seriously hurt himself. His knee was a little tender, but he stumbled out of the car towards the Shell parking lot.

The car in front of him had multiple people in it as well. Two young black women, *probably just teenagers who are scared*, he thought idly, took off and ran down the street away from the gas station. The driver, a tall black man who wore a white shirt stained with dark red blotches, got out of the car and immediately slammed his phone onto the pavement in front of him, screaming: "Jesus! My fucking car!" He was tall, a little taller than Mike. He was a good thirty or forty pounds overweight, and young, maybe in his early twenties. His friend got out of the passenger side and immediately got out his phone, his fingers furiously texting.

People began to gather around; those from the Shell store, people in stores nearby, and Mike began to hear, "What happened?", "Did you see it?", "Whose fault was it?", and "How fast were they going?"

The ringing in his ear was still there but he absently noticed that his glasses were dirty. While standing on a small sidewalk he took out a black cloth from his pocket and started to clean them. He had the odd thought, *glasses are dirty, have to clean them*. He was perhaps a little disassociated from the whole scene. He looked up and saw fluid running from both cars starting to pool in a pothole just a few feet downhill from the accident. From the rented white van there was yellow fluid running out, coursing over the engine, down the bumper and onto the road. From the grey Honda was a blue trickle of fluid. The mixture on the ground was turning green.

Yellow and blue make green, funny how commercials stick in your head, Mike thought. That ziplock one was there now and at the strangest time. He had the thought that the cars were wounded animals or maybe even people, it was like their blood was draining out. Like these tangled metal beasts were dying and there was nothing any of these people could do but stand around and watch. *It's both terrible and beautiful*, he thought. *It's a weird thing how there is chaos around the two cars, people talking, cell phones buzzing, and I can hear sirens. The cops must be on their way. The cars though, they stand apart. The two of them now are just sitting there, bleeding out and becoming nothing more than useless hunks of metal, plastic, rubber, and wires. They are almost like two warriors that delivered fatal blows to each other, but at a loss, and both are paying the ultimate price.* His dad began to walk around. He was picking up pieces of metal, pieces of glass. Mike knew the man hated to be idle. He saw that the smoke that had been coming from the car had diminished from a steady stream to just a few puffs of smoke. *Not fire,* he thought, *the gas tank is in the back. It's probably just the radiator or the air conditioner maybe. I saw a car on fire, happened to my brother's old jeep right in our driveway a few years ago. That fire started quick and burned hot and bright. This is a lot different.* He walked over and began to pick up pieces of glass, metal and plastic. It felt slimy on his fingers but he helped his dad move it off the road and onto the sidewalk. Lots of people were on their phones now and he looked up and saw someone he knew, Kathy, the woman who cleaned their room at the hotel. He was surprised to see her, but glad. She was friendly and was the only person they knew here on Eleuthera. Their eyes met for a second and he nodded at her.

Mike's wife came over, her face was flushed and her eyebrows were raised, making wrinkles on her forehead. He knew the look; she wasn't angry, just concerned and worried. She got close and whispered to him, "We're all ok. The driver of the other car is covered in wine stains, and the bottle is still in the car. I took a picture but you get out your phone, take some pictures too. Your mom hurt her arm. Kathy is going to take us to the clinic." Mike nodded.

"Yes, sure, that's a good idea. I'll take some pictures. Look...I'm sorry, I feel terrible. Are you sure you're ok?" He reached out and laid a hand on her shoulder.

Nicole's eyes looked full but she did not cry. "It's alright. Luckily no one is badly hurt. I'm fine. Just keep checking your phone, ok? Look after your father, and I'll text you when we get settled away. I love you."

He let his hand drop and whispered back "I love you too, we'll all be fine. I'll be sure to check my phone." He noticed now that his mom was holding her arm and she had walked over with Kathy. His dad had moved onto the van and was starting to get the bags out of it. They had done some shopping today and had been to the beach, so there were at least six bags. He went back into the driver's seat and this time the key came out. He took it and helped carry over the bag.

A tall, young boy with a red shirt and shorts on came up to him. "What happened? Did you cause the accident?"

Mike knew it had been his fault but instinct kicked in and he decided to lie. It was none of the kid's business anyway. "We were both trying to turn into the parking lot. So I'm not sure it was anyone's fault, the police will have to sort that out."

The kid nodded and just said "Oh, I see," really slowly and then turned to his friend. Mike thought, *it's what you get in a small town. Everyone comes out to see any kind of activity, anything out of the ordinary.* Remembering what his wife asked, he went over to the other car, the driver was somewhere off to the side and MIke took the picture, there was indeed a large bottle of wine just sitting on the floor on the passenger side. He took several pictures. He figured that the cops, along with the rental and insurance companies might want them.

The cops finally got there, the sun had almost set and he noticed one car, a jeep, turned on its light from the direction of the grey Honda and another car—a more traditional cruiser cop car—lightened up the scene from behind the white van. The two officers were going around, talking to people. Then one of them started to take pictures while the other one put chalk markings on the road. Looking at the paint job on the side of the van which read, *Big Jimmy's Rental Cars*, Mike realized that he had to call the company to let them know what had happened.

He punched in the numbers and a woman's voice answered, "Hello, this is Kristen at Big Jimmy's, how can I help you?"

Mike was suddenly nervous. "Oh, um, hi. This is Mike, we...I mean I rented a car from you on

Saturday. This is Mike Dwyer. I'm afraid we've been in an accident and the car is wrecked."

He could hear the concern in the woman's voice, "You've what? Oh I'm sorry to hear that. How bad is it? Can you get the car off the road? Are the police there now?"

He looked over and saw that his dad had brought over two more bags from the van. One of the police, a shorter man with a large belly, was motioning for him to come forward. "Look, one of the cops needs to talk to me. So yes, they are here now." The cop glanced at Mike, then went back to writing in his notebook.

"Did the airbags work?"

"Yes the airbags went off."

"Did you hit the other car head on?"

"Yes, we hit head on."

"What happened with our rental van next?"

"It started to smoke and lots of fluid ran out of it." Mike rubbed the bridge of his nose, closed his eyes and let out a long sigh.

"Can you get the van to start? Is it badly damaged?"

"No, It won't start. Yes, would say it's badly damaged. You'll need to send us another car please, it was insured and we have to get back to the airport on Monday."

"Well it's a Saturday night." she replied, sounding more businesslike, but still helpful. "There is no way I can get another car to you tonight. It will be tomorrow after lunch. Where are you staying? Can you get our van off the road?"

"We are at Shoal Point Inn on the Queen's Highway, just outside of Governor's Harbour. Yes, sure, tomorrow after lunch is fine. I guess we can try to push it off the road, there is a little dirt lot nearby." His father was with the police officer now, so he had another moment or two.

"Call me back with the officer's name and number, please. I'll need it for the insurance. Are you all ok? Do you need medical assistance?"

Mike looked around, noticing all the bags were piled up and the two teenagers were still hanging around, it was almost dark now and despite the headlights from the two cars, it was getting hard to see. "My wife took my mom to the clinic." As if on cue there was a horn sound. Mike knew that it was a text coming in "But we're all ok, just some bumps and bruises, thanks for asking. I just got a text from them so I have to go, I'll call you back."

He hit the end button and looked at the text: *We're at the clinic, waiting to see the nurse. Make sure to get everything out of the van. Kathy is coming back to get you, look after your father.*

Mike quickly wrote back: *Yes, I'll do that. Thank you for letting me know, love you. See you soon.*

His dad came over and Mike noticed that he was limping a little on his left side but decided not to say anything for now. "Daniel, they need to move the car. Hand me the keys." His voice sounded tired.

Mike immediately started to walk towards the van. "It's ok, Dad, I'll come over. I was just on the phone with the rental company. They will bring us another car tomorrow." His dad just nodded. Mike got in the vehicle and was happy to see that he could get the van into neutral. He got back out and helped his dad and the two cops push it off the road. A tow truck had shown up and was waiting in the Shell parking lot.

At the same moment, a black sedan pulled up and Kathy got out of the passenger's side. Mike went over to the cop who had motioned to him before. "Hello, officer. I was on the phone with the rental company. She asked if I could have your name and badge number, please. It's for the insurance."

He stopped writing in his notepad and looked up. "Oh, yes, of course. Officer Browne, badge number 442. Now I'll need some information from you. You were driving?"

"Yes officer, I was driving. The other driver was going really fast and I took a picture of the wine bottle in the car, I'm sure you noticed it."

The man nodded, "Yes, we will question him. Please give me your name, address, and where you are staying."

Mike gave him the information along with his cell phone number. "Look, I need to take my father to the clinic and my mom and wife are there. We leave on Monday afternoon. Please call me and I'll come down to the station and straighten all this out. I don't want to press charges. We just want to put this behind us." The lies were flowing, but at least the last part was true. Any good memories or feelings of Eleuthera he had here were gone. He just wanted to get back to the house in Florida.

"Yes, of course, sir. I will have someone call you Monday morning about our ruling. Thank you for your help."

"Daniel, if you and your father could come with me. We will take you to the clinic." Kathy offered.

Mike got his dad to stop picking up debris from the road and they got in the car with Kathy and her friend. On the way there he called Kristen back at the rental office, and told her the officer's name and badge number.

Pulling up to the clinic, he noticed that like a lot of places in Eleuthera, it was dirty and run down, with hot broken pavement and concrete all around the parking lot. It only had one nurse on staff. As the adrenaline wore off, Mike felt the soreness in his chest coming back. That, along with the guilt that started to fill up the bottom of his stomach. As if the situation couldn't be more awkward, the young man who had driven the grey Honda was sitting there along with a large group of people. Mike avoided eye contact with him. He sat down with his wife and mom. She was holding onto her arm and he could see the swelling immediately. His wife spoke up, "We've been waiting about a half hour, we should get in soon."

Mike nodded and looked to his mom, "Can you move your arm?"

She moved her arm and said, "It's not broken. Don't worry about me. Like your father always says, if the only thing we need to fix this is money, then it's not so bad."

His father rooted around in his pockets and brought out these metal and glass objects. Mike recognized them; they were reflectors that go on roads. He smiled and his father said, "Besides it's not a total loss, I took these when no one was looking."

Those are normally embedded on the road, Mike reflected, *I guess not in this dump.* This brought a few chuckles from Mike, Nicole, his mom, and Elizabeth. The nurse came out into the waiting room and pointed to them, then motioned with her fingers for them to come forward.

* * *

Mike looked out the window. He could see the green ocean and a red and white wing on his left. *Lousy sons of bitches!* he thought. *The guy was clearly drinking and they said they didn't do a breathalyser or a blood test, just took his word that it was his friend who had been drunk.* He let out a big sigh and allowed his shoulders to slump. *What chance did we have? Local place, no hope in hell they would rule against a local boy.* His wife sat next to him, her blonde hair had fallen down over her face as she slept. *Also, because they kept me waiting at the police station for an hour and a half, we missed our flight and had to take this later one. Now instead of six or seven, it will be after ten before we get back to the house.* He rubbed the bridge of his nose and closed his eyes. *I have to drive though, my parents aren't able to, and Nicole is too tired. I also have to look on the bright side, it won't affect my license or my insurance, and no one was seriously hurt. As we paid for the full value of the rental car with a credit card we may even get the four grand back. Buying anything with a credit card usually provides insurance. I'm a lucky guy, and in a few days it will be just another day in paradise for me.* He looked out the window once more as the plane went up and the view was obscured by white, puffy clouds. He closed his eyes and leaned back in his seat. *Goodbye Eleuthera, you'll never see any of us again.*

Life Model Copy

He pushed his blond, almost orange hair out of his eyes. *Damned air-conditioner!* he thought, *I'll have the house manager fired if he doesn't fix this soon!* The room he was in was cool, which was important as it was a good eighty degrees outside and he couldn't stand to sweat or be uncomfortable. No, not for a second. The rug beneath his feet was old, perhaps over a hundred, but he liked some antiques. It was light brown in color and had a castle in the middle surrounded by birds. The center of the room was filled with a bricked-up fireplace and small gold statues to either side of it. *Mar-a-lago*, he thought, *a great place, just great! Not enough gold though, I'll have to speak to someone about that. If Belladonna and Daron are going to stay here, they must get only the best. This is an important talk. Wilhelm had better make sure that the hackers are on board. That bitch Holly has pulled ahead in the polls. Well, if she wants to see who is truly great at winning an election, I'll show her.* He opened up his gold laptop that had the word FRUMP on the top, also in gold, but with white gold around the edges. The screen lit up, showing a picture of himself in a white sweater holding a tennis racket as the background. He moved his orange finger along the track pad. Finding the icon for Skype, he double-clicked on it and scrolled through his contact list. Finding Wilhelm Gutin, he clicked on the name and opened up the video chat window.

Immediately on the screen was a man with thinning brown hair combed over all on the right side. He wasn't wearing a shirt. "John! My comrade, how are you this evening? Enjoy the fine vodka I sent you?"

"Wilhelm, my friend. The vodka is great, everything is going great. Frump towers are making more than ever, I have more twitter followers than Holly. Arnold Schwarzenegger is in line to take over my top rated reality show—"

Wilhelm held up his right hand. "Let me stop you, John. Everything is always going great, but you're not telling whole truth. Holly Brighton is ahead in the polls." There was a noise from somewhere on the other screen. John moved his head from side to side to try to see what it was. "My security chief has informed me that the connection is now secure. He said that your laptop was fixed remotely, and mine has iron clad scrambling power, no one is able to listen in or record this. You are alone with door locked?"

John nodded, "Yes, it's a great lock, no one will bother me. I'm excellent at security, ask anyone."

"Stop talking John! You are like old hen sometimes, not knowing when to be quiet. I know why you are calling me. Have no fear; Russian hackers are ready to go with your election. We will give you more votes. Dead people, same ones twice, whatever it takes. No one will be able to prove it. Even if all that fails we have convinced those in your electoral college to stay faithful. You have FBI contact ready to act?"

John frowned for a moment. *Lucky for him, I need this favour. Arrogant piece of shit, cutting me off. If I get in, I could cut off trade, or send over CIA, there are lots of ways to deal with him.* "Oh, yes. Steven is a great guy, he was happy with my generous offer. Land, women, money, everyone has their price. The investigation into Holly's e-mails will be re-opened just at the right time to spook her voters. People here are so stupid, you just lie to them and they believe it. It's great!"

Wilhelm nodded and brought a glass up to his mouth, taking a sip. Immediately afterwards, he bit into a piece of onion and shook his head. "Ah, you should try this John, heightens the experience. Onion with your vodka, this is how it is supposed to be. Good, Steven will do his part, you will be elected in January, and you will play ball. In return I will keep video of excellent Russian hookers from public view."

John's face flushed, anger came into his voice. "Those hookers were great but remember; I watched them pee on each other! No one pisses on me, you keep that video to yourself and yes, I'll play ball. You remember to do the same."

Wilhelm took another sip and bit into another onion slice, grimacing for a split second. "You remember the same. You owe Russia big time, slip up and whole house of cards comes falling down. They call this treason, yes? You go to jail for a long time I think anyone find out."

The color drained from John's face and he lowered his head. "I...yes, Wilhelm, that is what it would be called. I take risks, I make money, I make things happen. This is what I do. I'm the most successful person you've ever met. Becoming the president is just another game. I will win because I fix the odds."

Wilhelm shook his head, and waved to someone off screen. "Whatever you say, John, just remember who butters your bread. I go now, five star Russian hooker here. She give me better time than any talk with future president. Maybe I pee on her? Maybe send you video?" He smiled then but his eyes stared straight at John, cold and sinister.

"No thanks, you go do that. I should check on Belladonna, we have lots of great, famous guests here. Goodbye, Wilhelm." Wilhelm just nodded and John hit the red hang-up icon on the screen to end the call.

* * *

Wilhelm closed his laptop and leaned back in his red leather chair. Before him was a man in a white lab coat. His grey beard was trimmed and he wore glasses. His face was scarred and pock-marked, and he wore a patch over one eye. He leaned over a table, working on what looked like a naked man with orange, spray-tanned skin. There were test tubes, computer displays, medical instruments, and some kind of electronic device that resembled a human brain in the room. "Dr. Prokhov, your work is progressing well?"

The man turned to face him. "Yes Mr. President, this Life Model Copy will be operational within three months. The other ones, who of course got pissed on by the future president John Frump, certainly passed the Turing test, with a golden shower of colors." He smiled, showing several gold teeth and several gaps.

Wilhelm chuckled, "You make joke and are stand-up comedian now? Do not be too confident over the results of that one night. Frump is not...what is American saying? Ah yes, sharpest tool in the shed. I want them tested again. It will be good test, if he can resist than he will be suitable for my daughter. If he does not resist...well then he will get a taste of my special hospitality."

Dr. Prokov's smiled faded. "These are not meant for killing, Mr. President. They are meant for sex and basic conversation. Their programming could not handle any special requests for Fassen."

Wilhelm downed the rest of his vodka and tossed the glass aside, smashing it against the wall. "I would not have robots kill Fassen! If need be, I will do it with my bare hands!" He stood and quickly strode up to the doctor. The man quivered, his knees buckled, and he would have fallen if Wilhelm had not gripped him by the collar of his lab coat.

"M-my apologies, Mr. President. I know you are strong, I did not mean to offend. A simple misunderstanding. Would you like a short demonstration of Frump model?"

The smile returned to Wilhelm's face. He let go of the doctor's collar and smoothed it out. "Of course. Apology accepted, good doctor. Yes, a short demonstration would be just fine."

He swallowed and said, "Right away." Opening the mouth of the Life Model Copy—or LMC for short—the doctor pressed down a tooth on the lower right side that was sticking up, and removed his hand. The eyes opened and he sat up. "Hello President Gutin, and whoever this is. Why am I naked? Are there some more hookers coming in here? If I could get one with blonde hair this time, that would be great. Jessica Drake, you know her? American porn star. Great ass, great tits, someone who looks like that. I'll grab her by the pussy, she'll love it! Oh and a robe, it's a little chilly in here. My phone too, I might like to tweet about it."

Wilhelm laughed and slapped the doctor on the back. "That's perfect doctor, shut him down now. The Americans will never be able to tell the difference. The real Frump will be here sometime in 2017 and we will make the switch then."

"What do you guys think about wire-tapping? I think I was spied on in my New York City office and I think it was the current president who did it. When I'm charge, I'll have congress get him! Yeah, send in the feds!" The LMC Frump raised his fist in excitement, then held his palm open for a high five.

Wilhelm rolled his eyes. "This buffoon is tiresome, shut him down, doctor."

The doctor nodded and said, "Female president." Frumps eyes closed and he fell back onto the table with a thump.

"Female president?"

The doctor smiled, "Two words that will never be spoken in Frump's term." The doctor laughed and slipped his right hand into his pocket, fingering something as if to check that it was still there, then took his palm back out.

Wilhelm laughed as well, turning away from him. "I will leave you to it, doctor. Clean up the glass, wouldn't want you to get a cut." He picked up a shirt and jacket hanging on the back of the desk chair, and quickly dressed. "Tell me something," Wilhelm glanced back at him, the doctor had a broom in hand and was moving to the broken glass. "How did you get him to act so much like Frump?"

The doctor began to sweep up the glass. "Ah, good question, Mister President. The internet and TV are responsible. Like many famous people,

Frump is on the internet constantly and there are thousands of hours of him from TV interviews and his reality show. I simply compiled all the data and made it into his personality. The memories are a little more complicated, it involves virtual reality and a powerful computer but also can be done with time. When Frump does arrive, I have a device to connect to his head. It will capture all his thoughts, memories and feelings, then a near perfect duplicate can be made." He pointed to a glass container in the far right of the room. Inside it was a black helmet-like device with multicolored wires connected to it.

Wilhelm put on his leather loafers, took a cigar out of his desk drawer, and cut off the end, only affording the doctor and his headgear a passing glance. "Very good, so that means you can make copy of anyone who has lot of his life on record?" He fished for a match and turned away, stoking the fire and puffing on his cigar.

The doctor now had the hidden syringe in hand, and moved quickly and stealthy for an older man. His hospital-type slippers made no noise on the tile floor. He got up right behind Wilhelm and jabbed the syringe into his neck! "Dexter," he said, "Such a good show, useful tips for me."

Wilhelm tried to scream. He spit the cigar out of his mouth and whirled around to punch the doctor, but it was too late. His strength left him and the doctor easily stepped back and let him collapse to the floor. "Yes, Wilhelm, I can make a copy of anyone. You'll find though that your LMC will have some specific directives, as will Frump's. Their programs will make me the most powerful man in the world."

The doctor stamped out the cigar on the floor. With a great deal of effort, he dragged Wilhelm over to the headgear, opened the container, and put it on his head. He then retrieved several large bags for taking blood. He put needles in Wilhelm's veins and got the blood flowing. "It will take some time for the blood to all come out of you, just slightly more than it will take for the brain scan. Russia will be strong again, my president, but I'm afraid you won't be around to see it."

☐

☐

☐

Section B:

Deleted Scenes

Author's note

This is an earlier draft of chapter one from my first book, *The Newfoundland Vampire*. For those of you unfamiliar with the series, I'll give you a brief synopsis. Joseph is a university student who is shy, geeky, and inexperienced with women. One night at a bar a woman approaches him. Cassandra, who turns out to be a two hundred twenty-four-year-old vampire, is literally the woman of his dreams. She is beautiful, seductive, charming, and yet deceitful and manipulative. She has also been trying to kill her estranged husband for over a hundred years, and she hopes that with Joseph's help she might finally succeed. Joseph has a lot of growing up to do and a lot of choices to make. Life as a young vampire is fun for a little while, until he realizes that there is not only Cassandra's ex-husband John to deal with, but also a vampire council with plans to rule the world with an iron fist. As most people would consider vampires to be undead, it is worth noting that my vampires are not. In the origin scene from the first book, we learn that the first vampire was created shortly after the Emperor Commodus' death in 192 A.D. A philosopher and magician named Galen cast a spell that brought him back as a vampire, a creature of magic. These vampires can blend well into human society and can, in fact, change their appearance and even gender given enough time. In the book as published, Joseph meets Cassandra in a bar. She has been following him and finally makes her move. But in the following original version he meets her in class instead. In this version, Cassandra has somewhat stilted language, which was later changed. Also worth noting is that this scene turns up slightly changed in chapter three of the final version of book one.

The Ring of Gyges

The structure was a strange place. It had started as a regular brick and mortar structure but then in the '80s they had built on a more modern part with glass and steel. The result was a peculiar sort of indoor courtyard where light streamed in from the glass ceiling above and you were able to see four levels of balconies on the right. The sculpture found in the courtyard called "The Red Trench," was something of a joke as it looked most obviously like female genitalia. The artist, Don Wright, said it was inspired by sand, waves, and the sea. But its removal from Confederation Building and eventual placement at Memorial speaks otherwise. The classrooms in the Arts Atrium were new and he liked how the plastic seats allowed you to lean back in them.

For this particular class they discussed Socrates, Plato's teacher and mentor, and the idea of the Ring of Gyges. Joseph found that he enjoyed the class. He had almost completed a minor in philosophy, but had never done this particular course. It was also an exercise in concentration for him as he had to focus on Locke's words, the red-haired woman seemed like a magnet to him, she always drew his eyes towards her. At one point, Dr. Locke looked directly at Joseph and made a swirl-like gesture with his finger. Joseph understood what he meant and turned his seat around. Just as Joseph turned, however, he noticed the red-haired woman wink at him. Joseph flushed as he completed the motion with his chair and felt twice as embarrassed.

"What would you do with a ring that could turn you invisible?" the professor asked. "Would you remain good and noble, or would you succumb to baser instincts?"

Someone in the front spoke up "I think that at first you would do things like stealing and sneaking into movies, but after a while your conscience would get to you and you'd stop."

Locke responded "Yes, good point, but what has created the idea of the conscience? Is it your family, friends, or is it society in general? Socrates would say that the most virtuous person would throw away the ring once he discovered what it could do rather than face the temptation at all."

Joseph said "In the Lord of the Rings trilogy," he paused, clearing his throat, "there is a ring that can turn a person invisible, and it is inherently evil. So much so that all the good characters in the books decide that the ring must be destroyed or its power will corrupt them."

Locke looked at him and nodded "Yes, I'm not familiar with those books, but certainly they borrowed the idea from this legend of Gyges." This led to a discussion about whether people act in good, decent ways because they are inclined to, or simply because they feel pressured to by society. He continued, "If for example I was driving in the rain and I saw one of you walking on the sidewalk, I would stop and offer you a ride. The reason I would have stopped, however, is not because I genuinely wanted to pick you up, but because society has imposed this collective guilt on us all that would make me feel bad afterwards if I didn't."

Someone in the class responded "Well that's nice to know," and there was a little bit of laughter. Locke, usually serious, did smile and even chuckled a little.

"This is a hypothetical situation of course, my dear boy."

"Yes, of course," the student replied with a friendly smile. Joseph felt this was a little off topic, but still enjoyed the discussion and found that the fifty minute class went by quickly. Joseph's parents along his with great aunt and grandmother were away on vacation in Florida, and he had even more time to himself than usual. He desperately hoped that something would happen with the red-headed woman. He felt so terribly bored and alone at times. His mind returned to the woman who had winked at him, he looked around and noticed that she had no books or pen to put away. More importantly, she didn't seem to be in a rush to go anywhere. Joseph wanted so badly to approach her, but what could he say? He slowly packed up his own supplies and wished that just this once, the woman would take the first step. To Joseph's amazement, this woman did.

She sauntered over to him and gently placed her hand on his shoulder. Her voice sounded like honey and wine "Good evening, fine sir. I couldn't help but notice that you glanced in my direction earlier."

Joseph turned around and his eyes darted up to hers nervously. He managed to stutter out "Y-yes, I did. I'm s-sorry, I didn't m-mean to be rude. You j-just have such l-lovely hair."

She smiled back at him, a smile which lit up her face and made her eyes sparkle. "Don't be silly, darling, most men would notice something other than my hair, and I appreciate the compliment. My name is Cassandra, and you?"

Joseph extended his hand. "My name is Joseph, it's a pleasure to meet you." He was surprised again when Cassandra opened her arms and gave him a brief hug instead. He quite enjoyed an affectionate woman, he was just not used to physical attention so quickly. He continued, "I'm glad you weren't upset. I suppose it has to do with my parent's business. They sell to hairstylists and I've always noticed a woman's hair before anything else."

"That sounds interesting, tell me more as we walk. I live at Hatcher House and I would like a gentleman to walk me home."

The canopy of the trees' leaves seemed like roofs of green that hung overheard as they made their way from the Arts and Administration building and across the courtyard by the Henrietta Harvey building. They walked behind Hatcher House, past the security building, the music building, and finally towards the concrete steps that led to a courtyard and Hatcher House.

Cassandra continued the conversation, "What part of the island are you from?"

"Um, I'm from Manuels, actually. I know that it sounds a little weird, but I really wanted to experience living on my own, so I decided to move into residence even though I'm only twenty minutes away."

"It's not strange, darling, I can understand your need for independence. I presume that your parents are well off, so I suppose that they help you pay for the accommodations?"

Joseph smiled a little nervously. "Well, I paid for my room, but they do pay for my tuition and books, so that is a huge benefit, of course. I suppose that being an only child I am a little bit spoiled."

"I'm sure that your parents are proud of you and are glad to help. What are you studying here, Joseph?"

He replied, still a little nervous and glad that she didn't seem to mind. "I-I'm in my last semester of my Bachelor of Arts, and I'm doing English and philosophy. H-how about you?"

She looked up at him. "That sounds like two areas that would complement each other. I'm nearing completion of a B.A. myself, in women's studies and philosophy. Did you enjoy the class we just had?"

They now approached Hatcher House and Joseph walked slowly as he wanted this lovely moment to last. Cassandra didn't seem to be in any rush either. "Yes, I found it quite interesting. The notions of good and evil and how our choices define us as individuals are fascinating concepts just by themselves. To add the dimension of a power such as invisibility complicates the notion even further."

"I agree that a person's actions speak louder than words, and that power is a temptation that would corrupt many good people. How about this business you spoke of, darling, do you intend to work there when your studies are complete?"

Joseph had heard this question before and as usual, he answered it honestly. "It's a good gig, and I have worked there before so I know it's not a hard job, but I've never enjoyed it much. I'm really not sure what I'll be doing when I finish my degree. I had thought of continuing my studies with a Masters in English, but it turns out that I don't have the grades for it."

A little frown crossed Joseph's face and Cassandra squeezed his arm gently. "I'm sure that you'll make the right choices, darling, life has a way of working itself out. Despite its appeal, the academic world may not be a place you want to stay in for too long."

"Yes, I suppose that's true. Schoolwork is an escape from the real world in a way. I did a course in women's studies once and aside from watching a live birth, it was interesting."

Cassandra laughed a little. "A tad squeamish, are you? I presume that you were in this class to meet women, correct?"

Joseph's cheeks blushed. "Yes, that was my main reason I admit, but it was also cross-listed with philosophy, so it did count towards my minor." Cassandra kept her arm wrapped around his as they walked up a short flight of stairs to the entrance of her dorm.

"No matter, darling, I'm sure that you behaved yourself."

She hugged his arm a little more closely. Time flew by, and he reached to open the door for her, and they stepped inside to see a group of people talking, listening to music, and drinking. It was a Tuesday night, but students at Memorial needed no excuse for a party. Some of the women nodded and said hello to Cassandra. Almost instantly, she and Joseph were each handed two beers; one for now, and one for when they were gone. He smiled and nodded at the person who had handed him the drinks in thanks.

Cassandra gestured to a nearby couch and they sat down. He looked around and saw empty plastic cups, beer bottles, wine coolers, paper plates, and chip bags scattered everywhere. It was similar to the standard condition of the Bowater House common room on any given night. He drank his first beer eagerly, still a little nervous, and found that the alcohol helped to loosen him up. "I've never seen you at Bitters before," he commented.

She turned to face him and smiled. "Perhaps I was there on a night that you weren't. I'm sure that I would have noticed you."

He felt his cheeks w

arm, wondering if she had just said that to make him feel special. "I go there at least once a week, sometimes nearly every night of the week when I'm not studying for exams. Of course," he added quickly, "I don't do a whole lot of drinking. I mainly go for the activities; movie night, trivia night, that sort of thing."

She shrugged and took a nip of her beer. "Nothing wrong with that. I indulge in a drink here and there myself. It seems that you really enjoy the social entertainment."

He cleared his throat. "Maybe we can go there sometime...together." *If you'll see me again after tonight.*

She smiled softly. "Sounds like fun."

He gulped more of his beer. *Can this really be happening?* He caught her looking at him as if she were sizing him up. He felt uncomfortable under her analysis. What if she didn't like what she found? "What's been your favorite class so far?" he blurted.

She gave him another Mona Lisa smile. "It's so hard to choose just one. What about you?"

He chuckled softly, nervously unaccustomed to a woman seeming interested in his rather boring life. "I especially liked the course that I took a few years ago in science-fiction and fantasy." The music was just loud enough that he had to raise his voice slightly to talk over it. "I've always enjoyed literature that deals with imaginative subject matter like advanced technology or fantastical creatures." She nodded appreciatively and looked him in the eyes as if she were genuinely interested in what he had to say, which was a first for him. As soon as the word fantasy came out of his mouth, most girls' eyes usually glazed over. Only his gamer friends shared his enthusiasm for the subject. "For me," he continued, "a good story transports me to that place and time, and the real world fades away. Though, to be honest, I'm taking a course now in Gothic fiction, which has been excellent, so I could have a new favorite."

He took another big swig of his beer and wished that he hadn't run off at the mouth like that. *Good grief! I sound like such a geek!*

She gulped her beer and slowly ran her fingers up and down the bottle in a suggestive manner. He noticed, and tried instead to focus on her words as she said, "I have always been interested in women who have been wrongly accused or mistreated. Did you know, for example, that women in Quebec did not get to vote until 1940? Far too late, when you consider that we gained the vote here in 1925, even though we hadn't joined confederation yet."

Joseph looked at her in stunned fascination. She was actually talking with him, and not ignoring his lame attempt at conversation. *This is hard to believe, I'm getting along with her, and she actually seems interested in me!*

He finished his beer, opened the second, and took a gulp. "Yes, I agree that the idea of denying someone the vote based on gender is ridiculous."

She drank more of her beer and asked, "What about music? Do you have a specific band or artist you enjoy?"

His head swam. Even though he had only started on his second beer of the evening, there was something about her that was incredibly intoxicating in a whole other kind of way. "Oh, um," he hesitated, "the Eurythmics. I don't suppose you've heard of them. They're an older group that isn't even performing together anymore. I love their music."

"Yes, I know Dave Stewart and Annie Lennox. They were a charming duo. I was glad to see them inducted into the British Music Hall of Fame. I enjoy listening to their music, although there's a bit too much keyboard and synthesizer for my taste." She glanced around the room briefly and then turned back to him, increasing the wattage of her smile. "It's rather difficult to talk in here, wouldn't you say?

Why don't you finish your drink and come upstairs to my room? It will be much quieter and cozier."

Joseph gulped the rest of his beer, coughing when a bit went down the wrong way. He didn't want to seem eager, but he'd waited a very long time to be invited up to a woman's room. Not wanting to waste a moment, he set his empty bottle aside and looked to her for a cue to follow.

Cassandra laughed softly and put her arm through his, pulling him up from the couch with her. "I'm on the fourth floor. You remember where the stairs are?"

He jumped to his feet and staggered a little, but she steadied him. He felt like a giddy school boy, almost wanting to pinch himself. *Is this really happening?* His doubt faded as she let go of his arm and led the way. He watched with undeniable pleasure as her rear swayed tantalizingly back and forth, daring him to follow.

Author's note

This chapter was changed drastically in the final version of book one. In fact, it ended up being spilt over chapters thirteen and fourteen, but it was originally chapter 16. It was decided at the time that this chapter was much too gruesome, and so the "body of evidence" was instead left at the crime scene. For those unfamiliar with my books, first see the note before "The Ring of Gyges". I will note here, however, that while it sounds odd for two people to always have swords with them, for my vampires, such is not the case. They always have swords. Cassandra explains to Joseph that other vampires, in particular her estranged husband, could show up anytime to try and kill them. As cutting off a vampire's head is one of the fastest ways to kill them, they both always have their swords on them whenever possible. This was actually not so strange for Joseph, as he learned to use a sword in martial arts and he is wacky enough to have one in the trunk of his car anyway. Another important aspect of my vampires what happens when they drink each other's blood, I call it a "blood embrace". Not only are their bodily fluids mixed together but also their souls and minds. It is the ultimate connection for a vampire and a way for

Joseph to directly experience Cassandra's memories. In this chapter, Joseph has made a terrible mistake. He had been resisting human blood but when he and Cassandra charge into a house and find a woman bleeding out, his vampire nature overcomes him and he drains the last of her life. Joseph is broken and it is up to Cassandra to do what needs to be done to hide their nature from the world. In this particular case, this means disposing of a body. I always liked this chapter the way it was written though, and while it is on the gory side, I'm happy to present it to you now by itself.

☐

Body of Evidence

Joseph's heart pounded with a mixture of fear and excitement as he drove the car a short distance and backed into the small alley between the two houses. He noticed in the rear view mirror that there was blood on his face and around his lips. He quickly licked his fingers and wiped it off as best he could. The blood had the same sweet and salty taste, but now carried no memories or thoughts that usually accompanied each succulent sip. He got out of the car and walked to the side door. Cassandra opened the back door and he noticed that she had blankets wrapped around the dead woman who was was slung over her shoulder. The pain in his throat was gone, but what had happened would need to be discussed once the body was dealt with.

She whispered only loud enough for a vampire to hear, "Good work, now carefully put her in the trunk. We'll bring her to CBS. You know an isolated place where we can get to the ocean, no doubt."

"Yes, I know a beach that is isolated enough.' He carefully put the body in the trunk in the fetal position to make her fit. Cassandra closed the door to the house and they both got in the car.

Cassandra laid a hand on Joseph's shoulder to comfort him as she noticed that his hand shook.

"Everything will be alright. There was no way to save her. Together we'll find who did this and make them pay, but now you must concentrate so we can finish this unpleasant task. I'm sorry about what I did to you, but I had to force you to act and you left me with little choice."

He briefly put his hand on hers. "Yes, I know. It's just nerve wracking and strange. We'll discuss what happened afterwards." He started the car and pulled out of the small alleyway. They made the turn onto New Gower Street and just as he started to calm down a little, his heart sank. Police lights flashed on behind him. "Fucking Jesus! This is all we need." He pulled into city hall and stopped in front of the entrance. He thought that if this cop wanted to open the trunk, this was going to get bad, real fast.

Cassandra remained calm. "Don't worry, his mind can be swayed and we can be let off with a warning."

As the man got out of his police car, Joseph cracked a small smile. "This one's mine. This is my friend, Vance. Everything will be fine."

The cop that approached had a buzz-cut of short brown hair, and steel blue eyes. He turned his flashlight on and shined it at the license plate before turning it off and coming to the driver's side window. Joseph was upset and his mind raced, but he forced himself to act normal, at least for the next minute or two. He rolled down the window. "Well you finally got me, Vance."

Vance chuckled. "I got you, Joe. Your registration sticker is expired, of course I didn't know that when I pulled you over." He laughed and Joseph laughed along with him, it was out of nervousness as he thought again of the trunk's contents. Luckily, Vance didn't seem to notice. "So this must be Cassandra?'

Joe leaned back as she extended her hand. "Yes, this is who I mentioned at board game night. Vance, this is my girlfriend, Cassandra."

Vance shook her hand. Cassandra said, "A pleasure to meet you. Joseph certainly loves his role-playing, he's already thinking about next week's session."

"Nice to meet you, too. So what were you two at tonight?"

Joseph replied, "We were at the Anchor Pub to see Ron Hynes. Don't worry, we only had one drink each and that was hours ago." This was a lie of course, but the vampire ability to shake off any signs of drunkenness included any smell from alcohol on his breath. Joseph had never gotten out of the habit of breathing and it served him well now.

Vance nodded and walked back to his car. "Yeah, I can smell the smoke on you." He coughed a little.

"Yeah the smoke is unpleasant. It must have been from the people outside."

He let out a huge sigh of relief for the second time tonight, and this time it was significant.

"It's good to have friends in high places, now we should really get going."

He started the car. "Yes, of course. We have to dispose of poor Jennifer." Cassandra reached out and took his right hand in hers. He drove onto the start of the Trans-Canada Highway, and her hand was a small comfort.

Cassandra squeezed his and as he did the same she said softly, "this is hard for you, I know, but it is something a vampire must deal with. It's better that you do it now, when you are young."

"This will be hard, but it's good that you're here to help me. Yes, that was a nice coincidence for Vance to be the one to pull us over. He's a good friend and a nice guy." She smiled as they continued down the dark, foggy highway. The lights on each side of the road near the downtown stretch came to an end and the night darkened further. "You're more to me than my girlfriend, but it seemed like the only thing to say to Vance."

She kissed his hand. "Yes, of course I understand, you are important to me as well. There will always be a special bond between us as creator and creation, even if you one day make your own vampire."

"The thought of creating another vampire has no appeal to me, but perhaps someday it will. We're going to Topsail Beach, by the way. It's off the main road and fairly isolated, but still close to the ocean."

Soon enough they drove through Paradise and then Topsail. He then turned down a small, narrow, somewhat steep road on the right. There was a small brown sign that said TOPSAIL BEACH.

"Turn off the headlights. With your vampire eyes, you'll be able to see well enough. We should go slowly." He turned off the lights and found that she was right. He had to focus, but he could see. He did slow down just so the car made less noise.

The road started off as pavement as they went by houses tucked away behind trees on the right and left sides, but it soon became gravel. They reached a fork that had a sharp turn to the right or one that was less so to the left. He made the left turn that led through a woody area and onto Topsail Beach. The gravel under the car made a crunchy sound as it went along. Inside, Cassandra, Joseph, and poor Jennifer, bounced a little up and down as they went slowly down the bumpy road. He pulled into a small dirt car lot up on a hill to the left, and stopped the car. His hands began to shake again. He couldn't deny what was in the trunk anymore, and he would have to deal with it.

"Give me the keys. The body needs to be brought down to the beach. While I get the body out of the trunk, stand guard and project thoughts of 'nothing to see here' continuously, just to make certain that no one notices us."

He handed her the keys, and they jingled a little in her hands. "I will do as you ask, this is just hard. That poor woman, we could have saved her."

She wrapped her hands briefly around his. "We'll discuss it more afterwards. This has to be done now or we could both have to deal with a fate far worse than being investigated by police." He steeled himself and nodded slowly.

Cassandra got out of the car and opened the trunk, retrieving her sword and handing Joseph his. He took it methodically, not sure why he would need it now, but in no mood to argue. He got behind her and projected his thoughts as he had been asked to do. She took Jennifer out of the trunk, still wrapped in bed sheets, and they both walked past the picnic tables and garbage cans towards the ocean. Even if anyone had looked, the fog would have obscured their vision as it rolled in off the sea. She unsheathed her sword and gently rolled the body out of the blankets.

A feeling of shock and surprise entered his mind. "What are you doing with your sword? The woman is obviously dead."

"The worst isn't over yet; a whole body could wash ashore. She has to be cut into pieces and scattered in the ocean." Cassandra brought her sword up to strike at the woman's neck, but he quickly moved in front of his girlfriend and grasped her wrist.

"This surely is not needed," he said. "We could just carry her body out to sea." Without warning, she tripped him and as he fell she shifted out of his grasp and brought her sword down, severing Jennifer's head from her body. There was some blood in the muscle and tissues, which seeped onto the rocks nearby. The sound was the worst part, a horrible squishing as the sword went through flesh and bone, followed by a small ting sound as it hit the rocks below. He fell back, slipping on the rocks. He landed on the ground, his own sword digging into his side painfully. Just as he was about to cry out, Cassandra was in front of his face, her hands tightly around his shoulders.

She looked directly into his eyes. "Pull it together, Joseph. Now that it's begun, we must finish separating her limbs from her body. Remember, you did this and now you must help dispose of her." He stared at her blankly with watery eyes and she said in a softer tone, "The head is the worst part, look away and focus your mind elsewhere. When the pieces are thrown out to sea, we will wrap the torso back up and carry it out to sea, for the current to take it. What I told you wasn't a lie; it just wasn't the exact truth."

He wiped away a single tear. "Let's finish this gruesome business. I'll help with the rest." She separated the limbs from the body and threw each of them in separate directions out to sea. With vampire strength, the parts were hurled far out into the ocean, where they quickly sank and were taken by the strong currents. He repeated the command in his mind as he was asked, and listened to each splash as a knot formed in his stomach. Once they stopped, he turned around and was slightly relieved to see that what was left of Jennifer was wrapped up again in the filthy, blood stained sheets.

"If you want to say a few words, you can. Religion is something that holds no meaning for me now, but for you perhaps it still does."

They took off their clothes and then picked up the body and carried it out into the ocean. Normally he would have shivered from the cool night air and the icy cold water would have almost paralyzed him, but now all he felt was wet and as the water went past his waist he stopped and she did as well.

"There may be some kind of God, but that doesn't matter. What matters is that whoever did this to you will pay, and hopefully now wherever you are, you are at peace."

"Nicely said, now let's get to your parent's home. You have a lot to think about and you probably want some time alone."

They let the torso go and shortly with so many holes in it, it sank. They both got dressed and got back in the car. He stared straight ahead and focused on the drive so he wouldn't cry. He knew that it wasn't a sign of weakness, but he felt that it was a private thing that he would rather do by himself. His bond with Cassandra had grown, but tonight had shown him that she was still capable of deception and violence. The gruesome acts she did, while he knew they were necessary, bothered him none-the-less. The excitement and terror of the night had begun to wear off and he just started to feel guilty and disgusted with himself.

Neither of them spoke on the way back to Cherry Lane. "I'd like to have some time by myself; I don't want to sleep alone so please wait up for me."

She kissed him softly on the cheek. "Of course, it's only 2 a.m. I'll just be in your room reading and waiting for you."

He opened the door and mechanically went through the motions of the nightly care for the cat. After he petted her for a little while, he opened the French doors off the living room that led to the spare room that doubled as an office. He carried on until he finally reached the sunroom on the back porch of the house. Once he sat down alone, tears flowed down his face. He sobbed quietly. Ginger somehow seemed to sense that he was upset, and came up on his lap and purred. He petted the cat and thought how his humanity had started to slip away from him. Tonight he had treated that woman the same, quite literally, as a piece of meat, with every last bit of blood sucked out of it. He thought that Cassandra had been right; he had made the choice to run to the house even though he had known the woman would be badly hurt. He could hardly believe that she had threatened to harm him and had choked him, but action had to be taken and she had made him act. He also knew that while he wasn't a doctor, there had been so much blood that human methods could not have saved her. He had never even wanted children, and now he realized that vampires could only reproduce in the strange way of creating another of their kind. He felt that being a vampire was hard enough and he didn't think that creation of another one was right.

His tears stopped and Ginger lay in his lap as he continued to stroke her fur. His thoughts turned to Jennifer's killer, the man named Green, and Joseph's resolve hardened. He wanted to make a difference in the world and he felt that the world would be a better place without this scumbag on the streets. He gently put the cat on the floor and she looked up and meowed at him. He had always known what the cat wanted and he knew she wanted to go out. So he opened the door for the cat and went back into the computer room to get on the Internet. He searched for different combinations of Green as a last name with Newfoundland as the place, but had no success. He searched by crime and street names, but still didn't find anything that he thought would lead him to this Green man. Finally, he looked for prostitution in St. John's and after some clicking on escort websites, eventually found a news article on the CBC website. It talked about how prostitutes and a john could be found near a certain united church on Gower Street. He printed the article off so he wouldn't forget. He knew that he was not up to it tonight but decided that tomorrow night they would hopefully find this man and show him that his behavior towards women was not to be tolerated.

He went into his bedroom and saw that Cassandra was reading a book. He smiled as he noticed it was The Hobbit, by J.R.R. Tolkien. "Nice choice."

She laid the book down. "I've read it several times. While it is described as more of a children's story, it's actually my favorite of the Lord of the Rings books. In particular the dragon Smaug is fascinating. They kill the dragon because he is evil and destroys a town, but the dragon simply does what is in his nature. Just like a cat kills a bird or mouse without thinking."

"Ah, but the dragon is more intelligent than a cat and knows the difference between right and wrong. He is taking pleasure in the action of killing others and that is what makes him evil." As he finished the sentence, his smiled faded and he hung his head down.

She got out of bed and came over to him. She embraced him tenderly and whispered in his ear, "We'll get him, but for now come to bed. You need a release from the unpleasantness of tonight, as do I."

He straightened up and wiped away a tear. "First off, we need to talk about earlier. You threatened me and choked me, so how can I trust you? Would you have killed me? I thought that you cared for me. I know you apologized, but I just don't know if that cuts it."

Cassandra did not get upset, she calmly looked at him. "You can trust me to do what is necessary and to protect your life with my own. Of course I wouldn't have killed you; I had to be rough because that was a dangerous situation. As I have told you, exposure of our kind is a death sentence carried out by me or by another. Also remember that you don't need to breathe, I took advantage of the fact that I knew you have not learned to tell your body not to do this yet. While you may not understand it, I saved you tonight. You may regret the woman's death, but you have an eternity to make up for it. Tonight was a test of our relationship, but I know we can survive it."

Joseph let out one final sigh for tonight. "I guess I'm not in Kansas anymore. I do see your points and I'm sorry to have doubted you. It's just that tonight it felt like a lot of my humanity slipped away and that bothered me a great deal."

"I know, beloved. Nothing in life worth having is without its price. Our thirst for blood and the temptations we face is the price for immortality. Now please let me show you how much I care for you, I need to put this unpleasantness behind me as well, at least for a few hours."

"You're my only guide in the vampire world and I need the release as well, let's join together as only we can."

She pulled off his shirt and undid his jeans. He couldn't help but be aroused by her sensual touch and kisses, and with her help, he did forget for a time about poor Jennifer. He enjoyed the wonderful release and intense connection that a blood embrace could provide. Just before sleep, his mind filled up with thoughts of vengeance. *The man named Green is about to see what a vampire can do. The bastard will never know what hit him.*

☐

Author's note

This is the fourth version of a prologue that I wrote for the first book. In this one, I introduced the vampire council in a much different setting. I wanted them to meet somewhere very secret and remote. The members of the council ended up a lot different from what you see here, but I thought that you would like to see how they appeared in an earlier draft. For those who haven't read the first book, the vampire council is a secret group that controls human society. For thousands of years their leader, the former Emperor Commodus, was content with the occasional world war and other horrific events. But now he has grown bored and wants to enslave humans. Fortunately for the world, only about half of the council agrees with him and thus, right from book one, I have planned for a war between sides of the council with humanity trapped in the middle. The council was a lot of fun to write as I explored what figures throughout history and present day would make good or entertaining vampires. So along with very creepy figures like Countess Elizabeth Bathory, known as Lady Dracula, we have the actor William Shatner on the good and less serious side. I love the notion of a group pulling the strings of society without our knowledge and all the conspiracy theories it implies. I hope you will enjoy it too. □

Prologue: The Vampire Illuminati

On a small tropical island located halfway between Africa and South America called Tristan, a group of hooded figures approached a cave. The island had only three hundred people on it and those few who dared or were stupid enough to be out on this night, shrank back in terror from the pale faces and fangs that occasionally shone in the moonlight.

The hooded figures all nodded at one another and entered into the dark cave. Several large blood-red candles to light it were further inside on a large wooden table. The figures sat down in their chairs and slowly pulled back their hoods. Their faces were instantly recognizable, and one in particular had a long greying beard and dirty hair partially covered with a turban that looked to be Arabic.

Another man pulled back his hood to reveal a neatly trimmed beard and dark hair pulled back and held fast with a cord. Underneath his cloak he wore armour despite the heat, and a bastard sword hung at his side. A third figure pulled back her cloak to reveal raven black hair and dark green eyes that seemed to have the slightest tinge of red in the pupils. They all nodded at each other, both as a greeting and as a show of respect. Each unsheathed a sword and placed in on the table in front of them. Soon from the back of the cave, a figure dressed in white gleaming armour, with a golden mask of a man's bearded face with a lion's head on top entered. He banged a silver plated staff on the floor. Those present immediately rose from their chairs and knelt in reverence before him. They all remain there until the masked figure said, "Rise my subjects and return to the table, let this meeting begin. Count, you may be the first to speak."

The man spoke with a strong middle-eastern accent, "Thank you my liege. My plans to spread terror across the world continue. Where once I led an army of Germans personally, now I must be realistic and stay out of the fighting. Wars are not fought with people charging into battle now; they are fought in the shadows or with superior weapons. I will be safe in a cave with my followers while soldiers die by the hundreds, and billions of dollars will be spent trying to find us! I will laugh and release recordings claiming that I am responsible for all terrorist attacks against them. I could never risk discovery with so many digital cameras and other technology around. These foolish Islamic fanatics believe that killing infidels is worth dying for. The world will know fear, and I will know satisfaction in these long years!"

Commodus sighed, "My dear Count, you are second only to me in age, and yet you choose to hide in caves like a rat with insane militants. When you were Hitler, at least you got to march into occupied cities and witness the destruction you caused first hand. Now as you say, you only strike from the shadows and let others witness the horrors."

The count angrily slammed his hand down on the table, causing chips of wood to splinter and fly off. "I remain committed to spreading fear, death, and destruction as I have always done! The means matter not, only the outcomes!"

Commodus made a slight nod with his head and said, "Yes Count, you are committed to your ideals as you have always been, for that I do admire you. As long as you are never discovered, the future results are approved." He gestured with his staff towards the armoured man. "Speak, Baron de Rais, what news of our kind?"

The man nodded in acknowledgement and spoke with a French accent. "Vampires remain a secret to the world and our numbers remain at a manageable figure. John Snow of Newfoundland continues to hunt others of our kind, but he kills no one of importance. Of more interest to you, my liege, is the fact that his estranged wife, Catherine, is about to make another of our kind. Joseph is his name, as I recall. Also as you may remember, ten years ago she made a youngling only to have him killed by John Snow. I am certain that John will seek her and her new companion out and he will kill

Joseph; such has been his behaviour for over one hundred sixty years."

Commodus responded, "A new youngling is always interesting. I myself will fight two young vampires later tonight; make sure two more are made in the next few weeks. John Snow is at least a man you can admire; he has always been obsessed with personal power over others and his encounters are always fun to watch. The sight of blood always excites me. Speaking of blood, for those who desire it…" he gestured with his hands in a spreading motion of offering.

From the back of the cave, came a tanned man with a white roman style mask and a loin cloth, and a woman similarly dressed. They paused at each seat to offer their arm, leg or neck for biting to each of the robed figures.

Commodus continued, "Countess, I have a task for you."

Countess Elizabeth Báthory pushed aside the man she had been draining and stood up to bow to the emperor. "My liege, it is a pleasure to serve you." She spoke with a faded Hungarian accent.

Commodus looked satisfied and said, "Good, as you know I love to see a good fight. Make sure you film the latest confrontation between Catherine, John, and her youngling, Joseph. There's nothing like the sight of a vampire getting hacked up to get my blood pumping. I believe also that you have met her before, so it will be a reunion of sorts."

"Yes, I did over thirty years ago, though I looked very different then. She will not recognize me now. It was a pleasurable evening though, and I look forward to seeing her again, my liege."

Commodus continued, "In truth my court, it is time that we come at least a little out of the shadows. This Catherine of Newfoundland already knows of the count's existence and her behaviour over time has indicated that she can be trusted with our traditions and secrets. The countess will reveal her true nature to Catherine and Joseph, if he survives. When you do this exactly is up to you, but it will be before you leave the island. It is time that the small number of vampires in the world worked for us and earned the privilege of immortality, and the powers we vampires possess. Instill in these vampires the knowledge that we are watching them and that they must do our bidding when required. What their exact tasks are will be determined at a later time."

With this statement there were gasps of surprise and shouts of disagreement. The emperor stood up and banged his staff once asking for silence. "Don't even try to argue with me, the count and countess have already been consulted and their opinions are the only ones that matter."

A few more murmurs continued and the emperor looked around the room glowering at them all as he took his mask off. His face was incredibly pale and he had the iciest cold-blue eyes of any being in existence. He had a hard large scar that ran from his eyebrow to his left cheek, and coal black hair that was curly and slightly disheveled. He continued, "No more discussion! We are superior beings and we are going to use all of the members of our race to our advantage! Only the count and countess will be known of for now and only to those that we three agree on in the future"

Commodus banged his staff quickly twice to indicate that the meeting had adjourned.

All of the vampires exited the cave and flicked the two dead bodies of the natives back into the cave. They were completely drained of blood and the countess wiped her mouth as she finished her meal. Birds, crickets and mice could all be heard in the foliage and the moon shone on thirteen hooded figures as they went their separate ways.

The countess retracted her fangs as she spoke, her gaze turning to the moon, so large in the sky. "I've never been to Newfoundland, it should be entertaining and it's been far too long since I've seen a good fight myself. This Joseph is about to experience a whole new world. For how long, only time will tell."

☐

Author's note

This chapter ended up still being number five, and was called "On the Road" from book two *Killer on the Road,* but a lot of the details had been changed. There was a concern that it may have slowed the story down to have them swim to Brigus, a small town about an hour from where I live. I thought the description of the two main characters swimming is interesting and worth showing to you now. Obviously I don't have any notion that vampires are averse to running water or can't swim; they still need to know how to swim to do it. My vampires don't have to breathe, don't feel the cold, and have great strength, speed, and stamina, and are therefore incredible swimmers. Countess Bathory—the same one who killed children and bathed in their blood— has been sent by the council to visit Joseph and Cassandra in this chapter. We learn a little of the countess' history, like the fact that she used to be Leni Riefenstahl, a German woman who directed Nazi propaganda films. There is a rogue vampire, Donald Rathmore, who has been on a killing spree. Normally the council doesn't care what a vampire does but Donald has been careless in his killings and risks exposing their existence to the world. Therefore, he must be killed. The fact that Donald was also created by John, Cassandra's now dead husband, gives her and Joseph a personal reason to deal with him as well. Here we are also introduced to the idea of a magic item—a ring. The countess has been given a ring by the emperor that hides her presence from other vampires. In my world normally one vampire can sense another's presence from a few miles away, kind of like an early warning system for them. It also means that, in time, they get a feeling on each vampire's aura, so Joseph feels warmness and affection from Cassandra's presence but hostility and hatred from the countess.

On the Road

Joseph slept better that night. Even through the wind howled and he faced an uncertain mission with Cassandra, he felt good because he had abstained from human blood that night and he had made certain that all of the donors were alive when he went to sleep. He dreamt of running through the forest with Cassandra at his side. The cool air felt good on his face and the experience of literally leaping from tree-to-tree was exhilarating. He smiled as he looked over to see Cassandra's dark eyes sparkle in the moonlight just to his right. He ran up a hill and made a leap into the air, his arms out before him like a super-hero, when he woke up to find Cassandra snuggled into his neck. She kissed him softly on both cheeks and on his lips, and smiled. "Good evening, my darling. I trust that you slept well?"

He nodded. "Yes, I did. Thanks for asking. I was dreaming about running through the woods with you. I am excited for this trip and I will be glad to have some time alone with you." Her gorgeous, naked body lay close to his, and he moved his hands up to fondle her breast. He could still only use the right. The left hand only had small nubs that would soon become fingers. He also was pleased to find her side completely healed and the beginning of a breast on her left side. She rubbed his back and whispered in his ear "just an hour or two more to wait, my sexy man, I will make it worth your while, I promise." She licked his neck and nibbled on his ear. She got up and quickly got dressed, "No need to shower, darling. Go say goodbye to your cats and I will make arrangements for a hotel tonight. We can easily make it to Grand Falls-Windsor on foot."

Joseph got up and got dressed. "Thanks for looking after that side of it. I'll pack some clothes in plastic bags and an extra pair of shoes for us both. I will miss the cats, but I have to trust that my stand-in will look after them."

Cassandra slipped into her clothes and looked back over her shoulder as she walked out the door. "Everything will be fine, dear one. I will have someone keep an eye on the place as well, just to make certain." Joseph packed a few things as quickly as he could with one working hand. He wrapped them up well in two plastic bags and took a pair of boots for Cassandra and himself. She must have had them sent here as he hadn't noticed these bright red rubber boots until this morning. They were cute, and despite all her talk of not caring about getting wet, Newfoundland was a very boggy place, and these just made sense. He came out into the living room and saw Jake and most of the guards drinking coffee and sitting around the fire. The countess was nowhere to be seen. He greeted them. The men waved or nodded, all busy with their thoughts and coffee. He found Frank, who meowed to greet him. Joseph sat in the sun room with him and looked out at the stars. It was a clear night, and Frank curled up in his lap, purring with contentment. He whispered "I'll miss you buddy, even though we just met, I know you're a special cat." A thought occurred to him, Frank might be deaf, that would explain why he hadn't moved for the car last night. He snapped his fingers near both ears and got no reaction, confirming his suspicion. Joseph smiled and thought at the animal, *try not to fight too much with Ginger and I'll be back as soon as I can*. Frank, seeming to understand, nudged him and Joseph put him down to find Ginger. He went outside and saw Jake slowly doing his rounds. He called out in his mind to Ginger and to his delight, he saw her emerge from behind a tree near the old horse shed in the back. She could still run short distances and it did his heart good to see her do it. He picked her up and snuggled her to his face, something she normally would not allow. He then turned her upside down and stroked her chin as she stretched out her paw. He whispered out loud, "I'll miss you." Ginger tensed up and wriggled out of his hands, clawing him on the wrists. Joseph felt the presence of the countess and looked up as she leaped up from the bottom of the driveway. Ginger hissed at her and ran off. He spoke "She's only a poor animal you know; you could try to calm her a little."

The countess sauntered up to him and unsheathed two silver rapiers that must have been strapped to her back. Joseph took a step back and she laughed, re-sheathing them in a fluid motion. "I will not harm your pets, youngling, but they will have to get used to my presence, at least for a few more hours. Once your fill-in shows up tonight, I will leave and two guards will remain. Your body double doesn't come cheap, so we would prefer he not be harmed. You are packed and ready to go?"

Joseph, who reached for his sword at his side and winced to see that it wasn't there, let out long breath. "Yes, Countess, I am ready, I just need to grab my things. I have to trust you and this man, I don't have a choice. If I may though, I would like to ask you a question about the count." He heard the door open behind him and briefly turned his head to see that it was Cassandra. She had two large hiking backpacks and two swords, and she hefted the considerable weight with ease. She gave him a small smile.

The countess didn't look at Cassandra, but leaped up into a nearby tree to sit on a branch. The heavy tree covering that surrounded this part of the driveway kept her actions out of view. She continued "I will miss all of these trees; they do remind me of home. Oh, your question. Yes you may ask one question, but I make no promise to answer it."

Joseph cleared his throat and Cassandra came to stand beside him. "Well, um, you mentioned playing for the count at the Berghof, when you were Leni Riefenstahl. I was wondering, how was the count, Hitler, so to speak? Was it before World War II had started?"

The Countess turned her head to one side and squinted her eyes a little. "For a pitiful weakling, you do at least have an inquisitive mind. Let me say that despite his many flaws, if the real Hitler had still been alive, the invasion of Russia would have gone much differently, or perhaps might have not even happened at all."

Joseph smiled at this. He had studied World War II and the German army a lot. He had also always felt that the invasion of Russia was one of their greatest mistakes. "Thank you, Countess. With your permission, we will take our leave."

The Countess did her usual half-smile-half-snarl and replied, "Good then, off with you two. I'm certain that Donald isn't waiting around chatting." Cassandra did a slight curtsey and Joseph quickly followed suit with an awkward half-bow. As they walked down the driveway, he looked back out of habit to make certain Ginger and Frank weren't following them. They weren't. The backpack must have weighed a good sixty pounds or more, but with his increased strength he hardly even noticed it. His sword was wrapped up in plastic and strapped securely to the backpack.

"Why are our swords wrapped up if we are going to run through the woods?" he asked.

Cassandra smiled and walked down towards Manuels beach. "First, my darling, it's time that you experienced the joy of vampire swimming. I know you are a strong swimmer and we will run through the woods, but first we can make a straight line across the bay to Brigus."

Cassandra laughed and began to run down towards the beach, just as if she didn't have a care in the world. Joseph appreciated her levity and jogged down afterwards; he did love to swim and was curious to see what it would be like. It was nice to have a pleasant surprise for a change. They both reached the rocky beach and Cassandra stripped down to her underwear. She opened a side pouch in the backpack and stuffed her clothes into it. Joseph looked around to make sure no one was watching and did the same.

Cassandra laughed, not at him but a happy sound and said "Oh, my darling, you are so cute sometimes. No one is watching us, my love, and even if they were, so what? They would never see us under the water. Remember, you don't need to breathe. If this is too hard to accept, at least try holding your breath as long as possible."

Joseph laughed too; it was funny for a vampire to still be self-conscious. Cassandra put her pack back on and secured it around her waist. "The packs will slow us down a bit but just use your sense of direction and head for Brigus, I know that you love it there, and it will make a good place for a quick stop to change and maybe have a little fun." She winked at him and waded out into the water.

"I love that town and the old house. It's a great idea, thanks for suggesting it. I will do my best to keep up with you." Joseph did the same with his pack and started to walk out. The rocks were rough on his toes and the wind felt cold against his skin. He shivered as he got up to his knees in the very cold water and then forced himself to ignore it. *The cold cannot hurt you now*, he thought, *and this is something I always wanted to do.* Cassandra then slipped beneath the water and Joseph did the same. Once he let go he found that the cold really didn't have an effect on him, and it was amazing to swim like this. He could open his eyes and see perfectly. At first, there was seaweed and sediment around him, along with the occasional fish beside him. He moved like a knife through butter. While he was a strong swimmer, he had never been able to move like this before. He naturally did the breaststroke, the backstroke; he even twirled and circled around a few times. It was a huge amount of fun and an incredible to feel the water move against his skin so quickly. A turtle swam lazily by him and he smiled and waved. Cassandra thought at him, *I'm glad you're enjoying yourself, darling. I'll make this worth your while, I promise.*

Joseph remembered when his parents had taken him from their house to Brigus in their boat. It had taken about thirty minutes; he wondered now how fast he was swimming. He thought back at Cassandra, *I am loving this, thank you.* Let's see how fast we can really go. He concentrated on speed and felt the pack pull against him, but he only dove deeper. He easily went around the rope of a buoy and a sudden rocky outcrop on the ocean floor. He had not mastered the ability to stop breathing yet, but he did hold his breath for ten minutes at a time, and only surfaced then. He knew he didn't need the air at all, but convincing his subconscious mind and his body of that was another matter. In about forty minutes, they arrived on the coastline of Brigus and climbed up to a rocky tunnel on the side of a hill that had been used by pirates and smugglers long ago. Despite their slippery hands and bodies, he and Cassandra had no trouble, and laughed and smiled at each other as they got out of their wet underwear and put on some robes. The tunnel was a tourist attraction in Brigus as it was a rather unusual sight in Newfoundland. It was a fairly straight tunnel and one of the only man-made ones outside. It was a cold night and no one noticed two people who looked a little out of place in cloth robes and boots as they strode up "The Walk" with heavy soaking-wet packs on their backs.

"I've had such great times here in Brigus," he said. "Even around this tunnel in particular. I remember being here with friends and having a fair bit to drink. It was summer time, so I went for a walk around the community somewhere around 1:00 a.m. There was no one around and I went to this tunnel and fell down several times coming back. I was drunk and happy though and didn't feel any pain. I'm glad now to be able to share this place with you."

Cassandra reached out to hold his hand. "You are such a dear, sweet man. Thank you for sharing that, my darling. I am glad to be here as well. We'll only stay for a short while, as I want you to also experience the pleasure of running through the woods. But first, let's see this house you've spoken of." They finished the short walk and came to a two-story house that was white with a black roof and a bright red door. The sign on the fence said *Welcome Friends*. Cassandra smiled as Joseph opened the metal gate and led her down the walkway to the front door. "This is a lovely house, darling, I can see why you like it here so much, it's very quaint with a pleasant homely feel to it."

Joseph leaned in and gave her a quick kiss. "Thank you. You know how much I love older houses. Let me get the key and we'll go inside." He retrieved the key from behind a mop propped up against a stone wall. The door creaked as it opened, and they stepped inside. The porch had a metal chain attached to a light overhead, and out of habit, Joseph reached up to turn it on. To the left was a spare kitchen and to the right a trunk where wood was kept. The floor was all painted brown but the wood had many different shapes and sizes as if it had been built and repaired many times. The floor was terribly uneven and you could easily see how the window frame was slanted as they walked into the main kitchen. Joseph went over to the large old-fashioned oil stove and started to light it. He was breathing and he could see his breath inside. "My darling, it's not necessary to start a fire, just think about feeling warm and you will be. Of course the best way to warm up is to embrace me. Drop your robe and let us join our blood together." Joseph did as she asked and she eagerly bit into his neck. He felt the sensations as intensely as ever, and he soon brought down his fangs and sank them into her neck as well. Her flesh was cold and wet but still soft and they slid down to the floor together in each other's arms.

What seemed like an eternity lasted only about ten minutes. Cassandra released her teeth from his flesh, licked the remaining blood from his neck and chest, and kissed him deeply. Joseph held her close, "That was wonderful as always, thank you."

Cassandra smiled as she gently released him from her arms and started to dig through the packs. "You're welcome, my darling, embracing you is always a joy to me as well."

Joseph put his own robe away and kissed her once more on the forehead. He let out a sigh of relief "I can no longer feel the Countess."

She produced a bright red plastic bag for each of them and began to dress herself. She put on dark jeans, a grey sweat shirt and a blue polar fleece jacket. Joseph also noticed that she quickly pinned her hair up and produced two new pairs of sneakers from a purple bag. "Yes, it is a pleasure to be rid of her. A present for you, darling, new hiking shoes with no laces, I know how you dislike them."

Joseph smiled and finished dressing. "Thank you, that was very thoughtful. So I'll just head west until I reach the coast, and then north?"

She laced up her sneakers and put on her pack, checking to make sure her sword was secure. "Yes darling, just remember not to run faster than a human when anyone can see you. Once we reach deeper words, you can really let loose and our speed will greatly increase. We should reach Grand Falls-Windsor just before dawn. I'll be right with there with you."

Joseph finished getting reading and clapped his hands together, excitement filling him up. "Okay then, let's get moving!" The two of them exited the house, Joseph was certain to lock the door and place the key back behind the mop. This time there were a few looks as two people ran through the town with two heavy packs on their back. Once they passed Roaches' Line and came into thicker woods, their speed became a blur at times, and Joseph experienced fully how a vampire could run through the night. □

Author's note

These next two deleted chapters from book three, *The Gathering Dark,* fill in some missing gaps in the story. For instance, "Anne's Vampire Birth" is referenced in Chapter five: "A Good old-fashioned Orgy," but was originally a chapter unto itself. In book three we get to see a lot more of Anne Bonny, a three hundred fifteen-year-old vampire and former Irish pirate. Anne had become reclusive and spent her days on a deserted tropical island until the day that she felt John's death. In my lore, when a vampire sires another it creates a tremendous psychic bond, they always know where each other are and can send each other their thoughts and feelings. Anne's greatest regret was making John a vampire and she was happy to learn of his death. Anne was also intrigued both by how John was killed—impaled by antlers—and by the two vampires she saw at his moment of death. Anne decides to visit Newfoundland to meet her vampire descendants. When she had still been human, Anne had been kept hidden aboard a pirate ship by the captain, her husband, Jack Rackham. Anne was rather wild and had a female lover as well onboard, which her husband tolerated. This chapter details how she met Bart Roberts, or Black Bart. She was seduced by him, and turned into a vampire against her will. When she meets Cassandra, they have a brief confrontation where Anne shows dominance, and she shares how she was turned with Cassandra in a blood embrace. Cassandra is able to witness how she was also made into a vampire against her will and they put their differences aside.

Anne's Vampire Birth

The sea was angry that day and the waves pounded against the Revenge. Anne had to take the bottle away from her husband Jack. It wasn't the time to celebrate. She steered the ship with a limited crew, most of which were below deck. The journey from Cuba to Florida normally only took two to three days if the wind helped. For the first day the wind had been with them, but now the voyage was like pulling teeth.

"Hard to starboard!" Jack yelled as a wave approached and she frantically turned the wheel. It was almost dawn and she was exhausted. As the grey light of day slowly broke over the horizon, she felt her hopes rise only to have them dashed once more. Another ship approached with the Jolly Roger flapping briskly in the wind. Anne knew that normally they could outrun such a large ship but with the sails damaged they were only at half their speed, Anne was enjoying her life as a pirate; fine clothes, fine rum, a man and woman to share her bed, the thrill of combat, and the respect of the crew. Yes, she had had some close calls, and had even lost her left pinky toe to an English sailor, but she wouldn't trade the pirate life for anything. She supposed that she had been lucky not to have met another ship of buccaneers, but her luck had finally run out.

Hours later, the storm had long since passed, and Anne and Mary were holed up in Jack's cabin. Anne suspected that once Jack had given the other pirates what they wanted, they had put their differences aside, because the shouting had stopped and there was jovial laughter drifting to them.

Jack, Mary, and Anne had an unusual crew. Most pirates would not tolerate women on board and that was why they had to stay below deck as soon as the storm passed as they could be easily spotted by the crew or another ship. It had turned out to have not been just one ship after all, but a fleet of them, some fourteen in total. They were lucky that the fleet had not just set them ablaze for sport. Anne had known of pirates like Bart Roberts, who killed people for fun. She and Mary had fooled around for a while; she liked women just as much as men, but she was bored now. The window on the back wall showed much gentler waves outside, and they were close enough to shore that she could even make out the land; it could be only a few miles away. A few lights from houses dotted the coastline like tiny stars. She felt both queasy and thirsty from so long below deck, and she paced the room as Mary slept on the bed.

Anne exited the room, and with no one around, went to the galley. Moving up to a porthole, she saw a much larger ship attached to theirs. She tried to count the cannons, but gave up. Her limited view made it impossible, but she was certain there were at least twenty. She struck upon an idea that would end her boredom. She would put on some of Jack's clothes and go on deck. She could claim to be pirate who had been terribly sick and not feeling right. The crew wouldn't dispute it and Jack would make sure that the story stuck. Luckily, she had small breasts and used a sash to bind them. Putting on trousers, her cutlass, and even smudging a little pipe ash around her face, she headed up top.

All the men were drinking and talking. Some were playing dice, and some cards. Obviously the rules that were normally followed on board were relaxed for the night, but she dared not reveal herself. Quickly, she spotted Jack. He was talking with a man who was almost a foot taller than him. A golden pommel at his belt, heavy gold chains, and a diamond cross around his neck indicated that he must be wealthy. He was a handsome man with dark hair, a short beard, and dark eyes. Finally noticing Anne, Jack's eyes widened that then narrowed to slits.

"Captain Jack," the man said, "who is this fine member of your crew? I don't recall meeting him yet."

Jack cleared his throat and thought quickly "This is Andrew, Andrew Falon. He only joined the crew a week ago, and doesn't have his sea legs yet, got an awful upset belly during the storm and must only just be feeling better." Anne nodded and tried to put on a deep voice. "Yeah, that's right, Captain. I'm fine now."

"Fine now, are you?" Jack said testily, glaring at Anne as if trying to burn a hole through her with his eyes. The other man cleared his throat roughly and Jack immediately changed his tone. "Oh…um, my apologies. This is Captain Bartholomew Roberts of the Royal Fortune."

The other pirate extended his hand. "A pleasure to meet you, Andrew." His grip was like cold steel. Anne was sure that he could have easily broken every bone in her hand. But his eyes drew her in; she was under some kind of spell, and stared at him.

"Good to meet you too, Captain," Anne responded in as gruff a voice as she could manage. She sensed her willpower, her sense of self, start to slip away around this man. He was hypnotic, entrancing, and yet somehow dark and a little scary.

Bart turned to Jack and sniffed the air. "Captain Jack, I would like to go below deck. There may be some finer brew for this special occasion perhaps?"

Other members of Bart's crew turned toward the stranger and eyes lifted up for a moment but with drink flowing they quickly returned to their activities.

Jack cleared his throat and his eyes moved back and forth between them a little nervously. "Yes, of course, Captain Bart. I'm sure Andrew will show you where it is."

Jack's eyes locked with Anne's for a moment, revealing disappointment and concern, but she remained defiant and soon broke off the connection. Bart's boots thumped on the wooden boards as they descended, and she could sense his hot breath on her neck as he walked close behind her. Her chest began to rise quickly up and down in fear; she had no clue what would happen next.

The floorboards creaked as they walked through the mostly abandoned deck below. The pounding of Anne's heart filled up her ears, and the *clump, clump*, of boots only dimly registered in her mind.

He must know, why else would he bring me down here? Her hand moved to her sword for the first time and finally Bart spoke. "There'll be no need of that, dearie. I know who and what you are. And besides, to be frank, you don't stand a chance against me. So now take off that ridiculous disguise."

Anne opened her mouth to speak but thought better of it.

How did he know? Either way I better get in the cabin, Mary can help me if I'm in trouble. She opened the door to Jack's cabin and went inside. She looked towards the closet, knowing that's where Mary would hide. Her eyes opened wide, Mary's feet did not poke out from below; she was on her own. She went to the bowl of water by the bed, washed her face and took her hair down.

Bart smiled and began to take off his shirt. "It's rather stuffy in here, don't you think?"

Anne wasn't sure what to do. Bart moved to lock the cabin door and laid his sword and pistol against the far wall before casually taking a seat at the desk. He certainly wasn't intent on hurting her.

He began to fill his pipe and his eyes meet hers. "Oh, and I'll have that drink. I know Jack must keep something down here away from the crew."

Anne found herself staring at his chest. He was not filthy as most of the men were. His chest was pale but lightly covered in dark hair which accentuated his chiseled stomach and firm chest. He caught her eyeing him and smiled. His eyes once more made her calm.

"You are clever, Captain," she replied, "And yes, I'll pour us both a glass of rum."

Snatching the bottle from behind the bed, she retrieved two glasses from a desk drawer. The bulge in his trousers made her smile as she poured the drinks.

"Please, call me Bart," he invited. He raised his glass and clinked it against hers, took a drink, then peered at her from over the rim. "Do you like what you see?" he added seductively.

She nodded, the booze combined with her intentions and his calm demeanor melted away any reservations she had. She wanted to do something wild and naughty. Downing her drink, she leaned over. "May I touch?"

His eyes never left hers and she could sense that he wanted her to continue. She laid the empty glass on the floor and began to rub his chest. His skin was surprisingly cool and the firm muscles underneath were pleasant. He closed his eyes and continued to nurse his drink. Her hands drifted down to his stomach, also firm and taut, before she gently scratched with her nails along his sides. He let out a gasp and his pants tightened further. His eyes met hers again and the world shrank to only the two of them.

"You are far too beautiful to be a man. Lie back on the bed and let me see all of you."

Anne quickly removed her shirt and pants, lying back naked. Bart poured her another drink and she took it gladly. He took a swig from the bottle and grasped her hair with his right hand, pulling her in close. Anne let out a gasp of surprise and pain. *He's strong, but he can't hold out much longer.*

Alarm crept into her head just for a second, but as Bart released her head and poured rum over her body, the feeling of dread went away. He began to lick from the tip of her nose all the way down her body, cleaning the rum off with his tongue. She had never been treated this way by Jack. It was what she had always hoped would happen; a sexual adventure and a man who could teach her, show her acts she had not imagined. His hands went to her breasts and squeezed them as his tongue worked its way all over her body. She began to rise and fall with desire, her chest heaving and her breath coming in gasps. He spread her legs open and her eyes widened in surprise.

"I...no man has ever done that!" she stammered.

He gave her an intense glare that silenced her. For a split second she thought she saw a flash of red in his eyes, but dismissed it as his tongue began to explore inside her. *The moonlight reflecting off the water makes strange tricks of the light sometimes*, she thought as she downed her second glass of rum. She was so lost in the moment that she didn't have a chance to scream when he bit into her leg. The pain came at the same moment she was about to climax, and her brain took a moment to process it. She started to scream, but Bart's hand was firmly over her mouth and it came out muffled. Any attempt she made to budge it was utterly pointless. Her mind raced and she thought of how foolish she had been, trusting this pirate and throwing away Jack's love. She was sure she would pay with her life.

Then, in an instant, he stopped and pleasure returned. He resumed the ministrations with his tongue and his hand left her mouth. He had removed his pants and had climbed onto the bed.

"You bit me!" she snapped. "What are you trying to do? I wanted you and you—" This time she was certain she saw red in his eyes, but somehow it didn't matter. Safety and pleasure spread over her mind as he entered her and once more covered her mouth, this time with his own. His tongue moved around her mouth and she responded. Somehow the passion she felt before had returned. He moved slowly in and out of her as her pleasure began to build once more. She had to accept that this was somehow part of his performance and he did not want to kill her. His mouth lifted from hers and she saw him bite his own tongue with teeth so long they could only be called fangs.

He grimaced. "Drink, and I'll show you a world that you never knew existed."

Once more, she felt almost compelled to obey and as the blood ran into her mouth, she swallowed. She closed her eyes as some blood dripped out of her mouth and Bart climaxed inside her. Cassandra witnessed the moment of transformation through their bond, the last seconds of her human life, and the beginning of another.

☐

Author's note

Gone to the Dogs, is a nice chapter where we see Leonardo da Vinci testing his robot war dogs. As this chapter discusses telepathy I'll explain how it works with my vampires. All vampires in my world are telepaths. They can read human thoughts easily, whether it be everyone around them or zoned in on just one person. They can also manipulate people, some to more degrees than others if they are weak willed. Two vampires can only use telepathy with each other if one created the other, unless they are in a blood embrace, of course.

Leonardo is part of the good half of the vampire council, along with President Obama. My vampire books are set a few years in the past. Leonardo, along with other members of the council, know that a war is coming and he is preparing. As he did in real life, Leonardo continues to invent and this time he is finalizing tests on robot dogs made to kill vampires. As with other very old vampires, Leonardo da Vinci has been other people, in particular a Roman sorcerer, Galen, who created the very first vampire Commodus through a spell. He alone has the ability to create and use magic among vampires and he intends to use it one day soon. President Obama is also a very old vampire and has been many presidents through history, including Teddy Roosevelt. The two of them are friends and determined not to let Emperor Commodus destroy civilization as we know it.

☐

Gone to the Dogs

Obama stared out at the ocean. He loved this vacation home on Kailua Beach. It wasn't just the weather or the incredible view, it was that he was near his childhood home, so close to where he was born. It was where his roots were. Michelle and the children had gone to sleep and he had business to attend to. Michelle trusted him completely. She would never ask where he had been, no matter what time it was when he got back. He already had so many secrets as the president that deception had sadly become routine for him. It would be a nice treat for the family to be here for Halloween. Natasha had turned eleven a few months ago and it would be her last year out. He closed his eyes for a moment and listened to the surf as it gently lapped against the shore. Peace and solitude were luxuries he would not be able to afford much longer. The state of the country was not good, and more importantly, neither was the state of the world. With people like the emperor and the count in charge, he knew that war was coming.

Opening his eyes, Obama released his grip on the railing. Although unknown to the world, Leonardo da Vinci was still alive as a vampire. He was still brilliant, and nearby. He had fought in wars; he had been Theodore Roosevelt once, after all. Despite what history thought, he had been able to use his sword just fine. The one that hung in a display case was a prop; the real one was always close to him. While his ideas had changed over the years, his resolve had not.

Reaching out with his senses, Obama located Leonardo. It was not far, perhaps five miles off, but strangely at least another mile down. He fingered the hilt of his cavalry sword. It was so rare that he got to actually carry it. Tracing the engraving on the hilt for a second, he then stopped. He used his telepathy on the Secret Service men, causing them all to look in the opposite direction while he leapt over the balcony. *It has been so very long, but perhaps soon I may get to use you again.*

He walked toward Kailua District Park and let his thoughts wander. It was well past midnight and he hardly saw anyone. He walked by houses and palm trees gently swaying in the breeze. The mountain that lay behind Kailua Park was already coming into view with his enhanced sight.

While he hated those on the council who would enslave the world, he did tire of the endless secrecy. *Perhaps someday there could be a peaceable way for us to reveal ourselves when those monsters on the council are dealt with, of course.*

The point became moot as the master, as Leonardo was often called, entered his mind.

Greetings, Barack. My cameras found you a moment ago.

Obama glanced around instinctively and put his hand to his sword. *I don't see any cameras, but he loves technology, so they could be anywhere.*

When you get to the park, the master continued, *you'll find three small stones on the ground. Press down firmly on the light green one. Make sure no one is around and then reach down and slide the larger stone slab to the side. The stairs will lead you directly to me.*

Obama nodded, out of habit more than for any other reason and thought back, *Certainly, Leonardo. I appreciate your concern for security and I assume that the stone is so heavy that only one of us could lift it?*

You assume correctly, the master replied. *I have checked the island twice and we are the only two vampires here.* Leonardo's thoughts faded from his mind and Obama quickened his pace. He was excited to know what the master had created, no doubt that this was some kind of lab. The sword clanged and jostled at his side as he jogged the last few hundred feet to the park.

Glancing around, he found it deserted. A wide open field lay in front of him. There was a children's play area ahead but of more concern to him were three small stones to his left and certainly another one hidden by grass. He concentrated, reaching out with his mind to check once more for another of his kind, and sensed only Leonardo. Then he did as he had been instructed. The stone slab was very heavy, over two thousand pounds, and he barely managed to slide it over so he could go down the stone steps. Once down, the slab moved itself back into place.

"Leonardo, you could have made it all automated!" he called out in frustration. He just managed to make out laughter from farther away. He wiped his brow and caught his breath. He spent so much time around humans that he had to blend in around, that turning off these physical habits was not something he could easily do.

The steps led into total darkness. He could make out the residual heat from the previously illuminated lights with vampire sight but a human would be lost in no time. He had to continually listen and reach out for his friend as he went down several passages that twisted and turned. Finally reaching the end of the passage, he stepped into a large workroom that was divided into two sections and lit by fluorescent lights. Leonardo da Vinci had on a white apron and had his long hair and beard tied back with small pieces of rope. His beard was tucked inside the apron. Obama admired that his appearance rarely ever changed.

"Barack, my friend!" He extended his hand and Obama shook it. "I'm glad you could make it. Sorry about the entrance up top. I have so few chances for amusement these days that I couldn't resist."

"All good. I don't get mad, I get even."

The master laughed once more and Obama smiled. Just to the right of them was a large steel table with a blanket draped over something that appeared to have an animal's shape.

"This is my prototype," Leonardo said and gestured with his open hand towards the table. "I called it the dog of war. I was hoping you might help me with a demonstration."

With dramatic flair Leonardo whipped the blanket off the table, revealing a black and silver robotic dog. It was about four feet long and had fearsome teeth and claws. Obama stared at it, moved forward then halted.

"Quite terrifying," Obama said. "Is it on? Can I examine it?"

Leonardo nodded. "It is powered down for the moment, I assure you. You may safely approach it. This model responds to my voice commands."

Obama nodded and inspected the machine. It had serrated, silver-tipped teeth, a long tail with a hole on the end, and silver-laced claws. The face resembled a German Shepherd with two horizontal slits just below the eyes. He bent over to carefully graze his fingers along the tips of the teeth and claws and found them all to be very sharp. Standing back up, he unsheathed his sword and held it by his side.

"I know what's coming," Obama said solemnly, "and we need to be ready. Let's see what your robot dog can do."

The master clapped his hands together. "Oh good! I assure you that I will monitor the situation and stop it if needed. I also have replaced the wooden stakes with practice ones for now. Please put on this test suit and enter the next room." From under the table pulled out a suit made of wire, mesh, and chain. It was no doubt designed to stop dog bites and perhaps weighed one hundred and fifty pounds. On a human it would be difficult to maneuver—for anyone besides an Olympic athlete impossible—but a vampire would manage just fine.

Obama donned the protective gear and stepped into the next room. It was padded from floor to ceiling and had a large bullet proof window dominating one wall. Cameras were mounted in each of the top four corners and the other wall held a solid steel door.

The master spoke again "Wardog, assume attack test pattern one."

The dog sprang to life, moving much like a real dog and nodding at the command. Its eyes showed a red light that passed back and forth from one eye to the other. Obama was reminded of the old *Knight Rider* show with David Hasslehoff. Perhaps he could rename the dog Kit.

The door clicked shut and the smile disappeared from Obama's face.

"Be on guard, my friend," the master warned. "I assure you that this dog bites. I also have given the claws and teeth silver edging, so take care." Obama swung his sword in several arcs, never taking his eyes off the robot.

"Understood, let's do this!"

The dog bared its teeth and growled at Obama in a strange metallic voice, shifting back and forth. Obama did not to give the thing time to gain any more information on him. He charged, but the sword came down on thin air as the animal sprang out of the way. It jumped over his head and raked the vampire's back on the way down. While the mesh had mostly protected him, there was now a hole in it, and he felt a trickle of blood run down his back.

This time he waited, crouched down low, and let the dog come to him. The dog advanced and Obama slashed below its left eye, exposing wires. A jolt of electricity ran up the blade and shocked the president, causing him to drop his sword. The dog let out a horrible piercing scream and Obama covered his ears momentarily. He knew that this was not going well.

A split second later, the dog recovered and came at him again. Obama just managed to roll out of the way and pick up his sword. This time, the dog extended its tail like a whip and wrapped it around Obama's foot. Electricity shot through him once more, but this time Obama gripped his sword tighter and managed to hack at the tail, cutting just enough off to free his foot and send the dog scurrying off once more. The metal coiled around Obama's foot became incredibly hot and he cried out. With his metal gloves, he pulled the coil free before it singed him further but he lost more of his protective suit in the process.

The dog was leaking some kind of fluid and was slowing down. It snarled once more, and this time opened its jaws wide. A red sticky fluid shot out and Obama leaped to the side. The red fluid caught his other foot as he slammed to the ground hard, still managing to hold onto his sword, but giving the dog an advantage once more.

Obama cut away the mesh armour as the dog tried to leap on him. With the distance between them small, Obama managed to thrust his sword into the robot's other eye, blinding it completely.

He called out in triumph "Let's see who the boss is now!"

The robot reacted instantly, as if this was part of its programming. It turned its head towards him and the smile left Obama's face. Its jaw opened, unhinged like a snake, and a large plastic stake flew at Obama, striking him hard in the chest and sending him flying back against the wall. He lost his sword and hit his head with enough impact to blur his vision. The dog's image swam before him in doubles and triples. He shook his head to clear it and began to crawl towards the sword. The dog's head moved around and not knowing his location, finally ran towards the spot that Obama had stood last. It slammed into the wall, narrowly missing Obama, giving him a chance to grab the razor-sharp jaws. Metal cut into his now uncovered hands and he smothered a yell as blood ran down his arms. The dog tried to bite down but the vampire managed to rip the bottom jaw off the robot.

Instantly, the door opened and Leonardo ran in, grasping Obama's sword and pulling Obama to his feet.

"Quickly!" he cried. "The failsafe is about to activate!"

Obama forced his feet to move and they made it outside the room. The door clicked shut. The machine turned bright red and then exploded. Metal shards, goo, oil, wire, gears, and other parts covered the room. Some struck hard against the glass, causing them both to duck instinctively.

Obama caught his breath. He had become so damned human over the past few years. "Well, now, I hope you have a change of clothes, as I may have soiled myself!"

"Oh. Well, I do have a robe in a bathroom."

Obama stood up slowly and clapped a hand on da Vinci's shoulder. "I'm just fucking with you, as the kids say these days. Seriously though, that robot dog put up one hell of a fight. What was he made from?" He could already feel his bones mending, but with all the silver edging of the dog's teeth and claws the wounds would take longer than usual.

"It's a titanium alloy, one of the strongest metals available, and yet not too heavy." He handed Obama a glass of water and pulled out a chair for him to sit on. "You have shown the weaknesses, though. The sticky red bacterial glue should be spread over a wider area, and the eyes…they are a weak point. Perhaps I could give them tremor sense as a backup? That way unless the foe left the ground, they could still sense them and attack."

Leonardo began making notes as Obama finished the water and got another, downing that as well. "Master, if that was the prototype with all its flaws, I wouldn't want to meet the final product. That would have been a wooden projectile from its mouth I'm sure, and I would be dust by now. You made that to fight and kill other vampires."

The master lowered his pad and tucked his stray gray hairs behind his ear. "You know what is coming with the emperor's forces. He doesn't tend to use technology. He will make others, many more. They will be vampires loyal only to him, who will be the foot soldiers in his war. They won't be a massive army, but a deadly one. Humans won't stand a chance."

Obama turned to the destruction in the test room and back to the master. "And these wardogs, they know not to attack us, and the ones who will join us? Will there be enough? Will they be ready?"

Leonardo put a steadying hand on Obama's shoulder. "I need six months, and I will have three thousand ready. They will be given facial recognition software, and they will never attack anyone I put in." He stroked his face and walked about the room. "Hmm, if I give them heat vision it won't matter if their eyes are disabled, for vampires at least. We give off a different impression than humans at night, so they will never mistakenly attack humans. Still, it's not perfect. They could then attack a friendly vampire. We'll have to deal with that when it comes."

Obama took off his shirt and laid it on the table. There was some blood on it, and he didn't want questions from Michelle. "Dispose of this please, and I'll take that robe you mentioned. Sounds like you have the situation in hand. You're right about Commodus. He wants thralls and we'll hope that the attack doesn't come before we're ready. Thousands will die, maybe millions if we fail."

The master went to a closet and produced a robe and a towel, handing them both over. Obama undressed fully and cleaned himself. Putting the robe on and fastening the belt around his waist, he said, "I dearly hope you're right, my friend. The spies we have in place may soon have news." He put on his socks and shoes, and then stood to shake the master's hand.

The master grasped it. "Thank you again for the help. We'll be ready and there will be much to discuss at our next meeting. I just spoke with Bill and he has hope. He just met with a young one

Joseph and his maker Cassandra. He is confident that they are two more who will stand with us."

Obama turned and began to walk back towards the tunnels. "I hope you're right," he said, looking back at the master over his shoulder. "As Edmund Burke wisely said, 'All that is necessary for the triumph of evil is that good men do nothing.' They will be invited and we can all judge their merits."

The master smiled as he showed Obama the correct passages back to the surface. "We will act when we must. The emperor's impatience and aggression will be his undoing."

Obama reached the first rung of the ladder. "That, and the fact that evil always turns on itself. Goodbye, and good luck."

The master nodded absently. "Oh yes, the same to you." He scribbled once more in his notepad. Once the cover was back in place, he added more notes and said to himself as he hurried off, "We're going to need it."

☐

Section C:

Preview Chapters of *The Newfoundland Vampire Book IV*:

War of the Fangs

☐

Author's Note

This is a chapter from my forthcoming fourth, and possibly final book in my *Newfoundland Vampire* series. If you don't want spoilers of the series you need to stop reading now, you've been warned. This takes place shortly after the events from book three, The Gathering Dark, in which Joseph, Cassandra, and Anne have killed Elizabeth Bathory, Lady Dracula. Not only is she dead, but Anne has changed her appearance to look exactly like her, something my vampires can do, and has all her thoughts and memoires. Elizabeth was not only killed, but also had every last drop of blood sucked out of her with three vampires invading her mind and in a way stealing her soul. The consequence being that now that Anne, who has taken Elizabeth's place as a spy for the good side, is finding it increasingly difficult to separate her thoughts from Bathory's.

☐

Prologue:
See What's Become of Me

"Time, time, time, see what's become of me. As I looked around for my possibilities," Anne was singing along to music softly wafting out of her Bluetooth speaker. She looked out at the sky and saw that winter was still there in Slovokia, a light carpet of snow covered the ground and large, puffy flakes slowly made their way past her window. She knew that it was delaying the inevitable; taking the Countess Bathory's place was a horrid task, and tonight was just another night that would turn her stomach and make her mind reel with what had to be done. She paced the expensive hotel room. She was dressed in a long purple evening gown with her hair and makeup done. It was quite ridiculous for 4:00 a.m. but she never knew when another blasted member from the evil half of the vampire council would call her, and appearances had to be maintained.

She fingered the ring on her left hand. It was a small comfort to her. Just as Elizabeth Bathory had felt, she too found it to be a kind of cool breeze blowing over her. The ability it gave for other vampires not to sense her was a huge benefit. She turned it around and around and looked to see that the one on her right hand was still there. It looked identical, she had made certain of that as her paranoia seemed to be limitless these days. She was not certain that she would be able to take it off now even if she wanted to. The ring limited her own abilities, she could not sense any other vampires, and she was unable to communicate telepathically with Catherine, Joseph, or thankfully, her own creator, Bart Roberts. She thought of Cath— er Cassandra, as she insisted on being called now. She was a beautiful woman, a good fighter, and a like-minded individual. She could see that humans were a curiosity at best and a nuisance at worst, so many of them would be killed in the battle to come. Cassandra had taken fiercely to this Joseph, her own distant relative, and Anne had to admire her audacity. The two of them were stronger together than any other creator and youngling she had ever known. Their human blood tie somehow connected them even tighter than the normal telepathic bond. In a way she pitied Joseph. Cassandra would always have him; he was like a moth to a flame and could never be without her for long. She had given him a good training, had loved him, and was a fantastic lover, with men at least. But she had her own agenda, and Joseph would end up following it eventually. Joseph, he was a pleasant distraction while she had been in Newfoundland, and he had managed to surprise her a few times. She never thought that he would have had a spine enough to agree to killing Anne and replacing her, but she had seen what she thought then was a wise choice. He could fight much better than any other vampire at such a young age should have been able to due to his human training and the blood of Cassandra. No doubt, along with a deviousness that she had not seen in some time. Joseph had made her laugh but she felt that coming events would wear him down. He was still naïve, and so very human in his thoughts. Those who take actions against evil, such as Joseph, had better be prepared for the consequences. She wondered if some pissed-off human could find him as easily as she had. She hoped that Cassandra would be there to help if that day came.

She absently tapped her thigh with one hand and the other brought the glass of sherry to her mouth and downed it. Alcohol helped, if only for a few moments. Her mind wandered back to that night in November last year, that night in Paris when Catherine brought the women up to the LaTrémoille. *They had had the blood sucked from them and at the moment of death, they had had their minds torn apart. They were made into these horrible abominations known as thralls; vampires with no free will, a slave to their mental programming and only good at killing.* She wished she didn't know how to do this, but that night in Paris she had watched Catherine— er Cassandra gorge herself on blood from the three women. There was so much blood and she...no, the countess had been aroused by it, relishing the task of making more thralls to serve her. The countess had wanted to take her clothes off and have sex with Cassandra while covered in blood. She hadn't, only because of her insane sense of propriety, and the fact that she had been so intent to go to St. Pierre and meet with me and put me under her heel.

She laughed. It was a small feeble sound, and she rubbed her temples. *So hard to keep it all straight*, she thought, it was so jumbled, like a washing machine always turning. It was too much, too many memories and emotions, all her hate, all her rage, her vileness. *It overwhelms me at times. What we did to the countess that night in St. Pierre,* her mind reeled. *We sliced her up like a fish. The three of us entered her mind, tore apart her soul, and killed her. It was such a wretched thing that we did and it had been my idea. It haunts me. I thought it would help. I could find out what these evil vampires were planning to do, and I thought that I could maybe even stop them, but I've only learned that a big attack will happen in September, not when or where. I even find myself speaking with her Hungarian accent when I'm alone,* it's...I'm...

Anne poured herself another glass of Sherry and paced up and down the lavish room with warm white rugs and hardwood floors. She passed by the bathroom with the large tub. Two men and one woman were on their hands and knees, with their heads leaned over the side, the legs tied to each other and to the legs of clawed feet under the tub. They were awake and struggled, but it was no use, one of them cried and moaned, the other looked at her with desperate eyes, the third tried to speak through the gag.

"Any thung, wal do anyt—" She slammed the door, unable to stand the look of them. They were pathetic. They could at least accept their deaths with some dignity.

For the first few months she had done what Cassandra had done that night; drugged them to the gills to reduce their terror, but she had long since given that up. Though Anne hated herself afterward, she had come to enjoy their terror as they died, the intense emotions her victims had let her forget the memories for a few moments. She had lived as a sort of wealthy vagabond for about four months now. She could never stay in one place for too long. She could easily fool any humans around her, but if Dracula showed up, or John, or the emperor himself, she just wasn't sure that she could pull it off with any of them. So she used up Elizabeth's fortune. She had lived in Paris, Madrid, Barcelona, Athens, Berlin, London, and now Trenčín. She knew that the ring hid her from other vampires but the council certainly had her phone bugged and some had some kind of tracer, so her constant moving around was hopefully imitating what she was supposed to be doing anyway; making these accursed thralls.

Traveling was something to keep her mind off of what she had to do every second or third night; kill more innocent people, make more vampire slaves to fight for her. She didn't want to confront anyone in the evil side of the council one-on-one. It would be too easily for her to slip up, too easy for them to be suspicious. Then not only would her life be over, but if they tortured her first…she shuddered. She knew what three vampires had done to the countess with minimal planning and experience, what these other monsters could to do her was almost unfathomable. *Monster, is that what I've become?* She poured herself and drink and hastily downed it. *There has to be another meeting soon,* she thought. *If they have one before the attack I can let others know and this won't have all been for nothing. I know from Elizabeth's memories that one happened last October, and that's the usual time. But this coming battle must need planning; it must make for an exception. During a meeting the attention won't be all on me, I can fake that. No, I'm not a monster, I'm doing what needs to be done. I'm giving Joseph, Cassandra, and others on our side time to prepare. It'll give them an edge when the battle does come.*

One of the good acts she could do would be to make these thralls fight for her alone at this coming battle, turn them against the count, the emperor, and that bastard, Bart Roberts. He had turned her against her will hundreds of years ago and had shown his true colours later when he hit her and killed the prisoners one day so long ago. It was the only thought that helped her get any sleep at all. She touched a button on her iPhone and raised the volume of the Simon and Garfunkel song that played.

Hang on to your hopes, my friend.
That's an easy thing to say,
But if your hopes should pass away
Simply pretend that you can build them again.

Hope. That was something hard to hold onto, something in short supply. But hang on she must. She hoped that wherever Joseph and Cassandra were, they were doing something pleasant; maybe having sex or sitting by a warm fire. *I miss sex, I miss being touched. I'm tempted to use these humans for it beforehand, it's not like they would remember. But not tonight, I haven't sunk that low yet.* As she strolled past the bathroom, she heard them whimpering. The ring cut off her telepathy but the sounds of these pathetic humans was impossible to miss.

End their lives, it will be dawn soon.

"Who said that?" she spoke. She instantly retrieved the silver dagger cleverly concealed in the folds of her dress and scanned the room. Her senses told her there was no one there, but the voice continued.

How pathetic you are, you hesitate and moan about every life you take, a whining sniveling bitch, like Joseph! The voice bellowed in her head.

"No! I'm strong. You're not real! We killed you! I drank the last of your blood! *Shut up!*" Her voice rose with the attempt to shut the sound out.

Her head became filled with hideous laughter and voice that nearly spilt her skull. *I can keep this up forever! Do it, spill their blood!* Watch them bleed out like cattle!

She lost control and let out a furious primal scream that turned into a growl. Charging into the bathroom, she got into the bathtub in front of her victims. Their muffled screams increased to a fever pitch and they all struggled with their bonds, pleading with their eyes for this not to be the end. Anne's own eyes grew red and with a savage snarl, she slashed with her dagger. In one liquid motion, she cut the throats of all three of them. Blood instantly drenched her and some gushed into her mouth, forcing her to spit some out and swallow the rest. Her purple gown was covered in red and she had to wipe it away from her face. An image flooded into her mind, then another, then hundreds, all of them were the same; the countess in a bathtub of blood, her innocent victims lying around her on the floor. That voice, the voice of the countess in her mind: *The blood, the blood is the life and it will be mine!*

Anne's eyes opened wide, nearly bulging from her head, and she bolted from the room. *I'm not her! I'm not her! She's gone! Elizabeth's thoughts and memories are so strong, they are trying to overcome. I can't let them, I won't!* Fortunately, her suite had direct access to the roof and she soon found herself in the crisp night air. She tore the blood-stained dress from her body and flung it to the ground. She reasoned that no one would be looking at the roof of a building at almost 5 a.m. and even if they did, she could use money and influence to quiet them. The snowflakes glided down and landed on her naked body, the blood slowly began to run from her face onto her neck and between her breasts. She breathed slowly in and out, trying to calm herself. She wanted to scream and she picked up the discarded dress. Clenching it in her mouth, she let out a smothered wail and looked about. Trenčín Castle was above her to the right. With her enhanced senses, she could even see the inscription at the base. It was in Latin and she didn't know it, at least she thought she didn't until Elizabeth's voice in her head spoke up again.

Done by eight hundred fifty-five Legionaries of the Augustus victorious army, who are stationed in Laugaricio. Done under the supervision of Maximus Legatus of II legion. Fortunately, one of us is educated.

Anne spit out the blood-stained dress fragments and laughed, it was the only thing left to do. "I can't silence her voice, the only thing I can do is try to benefit from it." *I have to go back down there and turn those poor souls; they have maybe 5 minutes until they bleed out completely. I can't let their deaths be for nothing. What I've done has to count for something; it has to help in the end. I'm still me and I can still help the world. I can still fight against those who would destroy it; those who ruined my solitude and made me hate who I am.* She wrapped the dress up with a small piece of rope left on the ground and flung it hard. It landed on another roof across the street. She never even noticed the cold. Blood was caked on near her stomach and she made a final effort to get it off her face. Straightening, she went back inside the hotel. She wasn't sure where the laughter came from, and ultimately forced herself not to care.

Author's Note

This is another chapter from my forthcoming book in my *Newfoundland Vampire* series. Cassandra has a lot to deal with. In particular, her vampire soul mate, Joseph, has been shot in a head and nearly killed. Only by giving him human and her own blood has she managed to save him. Joseph's brain, however, is just barely functioning and it has left him in a feral state. Cassandra must get Joseph back to her house and stop Joseph from causing further harm to himself or even killing her in his crazed state.

☐

Chapter 1
Don't Let Me Down

Humans! Cassandra thought as she trudged through the woods. The snow was up past her knees despite it being the middle of March. *After all the things Joseph has done to help them, all the things I've done, that goddamned pimp just couldn't learn his lesson. He had to seek out revenge.* She stumbled and Joseph slipped from her shoulder. She only just managed to catch him before he hit the ground. *Green had killed that woman, Jennifer I think her name was, and it had felt so good to thrash him outside the church.* Normally after twenty minutes of walking, she would have been at her castle in Torbay. However, her blood loss with the fight, and giving so much to Joseph had drained her. That, and the fact that he was out cold and she had to carry him.

She said, "Lousy bugger," and spat on the ground as her thoughts continued. *It was less than a year ago but things had seemed so much simpler. We didn't know about the coming war, had not met with Shatner or the other good members of the council. Of course, we did have to kill my ex-husband, but still it was good. I wonder if it was the terrible head wound that changed John? Sure, he had been a bastard to me for years, but as a vampire he had been just plain evil. His humanity seemed to have been wiped away. I can only hope that Joseph doesn't suffer a similar fate. If he does I will have to get rid of him too, but he's my beloved. How could I ever do such a thing?*

She didn't want to think of killing Joseph. She would get him help if it came to that, and she dearly hoped that it didn't. She stopped walking and gently lowered Joseph to the ground. She switched and put him over her left shoulder. She used her senses out of pure instinct. There were no other vampires within miles. A squirrel scurried about nearby and a rabbit was under a tree behind her, looking for warmth. The snow drifted down on her. A snowflake landed on her cheek and she absently wiped it away with her left hand.

Joseph might have finished the job with Green that night in October if I had let him. I had shown the man mercy and now it's my fault that he was able to hurt Joseph so badly. Any other human that crosses me won't be so lucky. I'm more than happy to play judge, jury, and executioner to the next pitiful cretin that does something reprehensible. He must have planned that assault near the airport for weeks. He was clever and resourceful, I will give him that. I wonder how he knew that we were landing tonight. How did he know to use explosive tipped bullets? Why did he have so many men just to kill two of us?

I suppose that none of that matters now, only Joseph's recovery is important.

Her nose picked up the scent of horses and she knew that they were close. Eleanor and Jake were mustangs; a female and male. They were in their barn with hay, feed, and blankets wrapped around them. She had wanted to surprise Joseph with the animals. She knew that he loved horses and had taken lessons as a child. She liked horses and hoped they could ride together in the woods or by a river sometime. Now though, one of them probably had to die to give Joseph enough blood, and she had to make the decision as to who it would be. She could hear the animals' heartbeats; a slow and steady, *thump, thump, thump*. She could smell their blood. With her own levels low, she might have to take advantage of the blood these animals had too.

She had been through so much with Joseph; killing John Snow, dealing with that twisted fuck, Donald, and the other deranged vampire in New Orleans. The horrible fight last November with the countess and her guards in St. Pierre had maimed her. She had never seen any vampire fight so hard and they had wounded her so badly. Then Anne had had to absorb the memories and feelings of Elizabeth. She and Joseph just had to dig them out and let them wash over her.

She finally saw the gate to her estate and gently laid Joseph on the ground once more. She thought again of Anne. She hadn't heard from her since then. She hoped that it wasn't all for nothing, that she was gaining info and working against the dark side of the council. Their greatest fight was yet to come, a battle for the fate of vampire and human-kind alike. She shuddered at the thought. Forcing herself back to the present, she got out her keys and hit a button on a small device. The gates slowly pulled open. Normally she would have leaped over them but tonight she just did not have the strength.

She walked slowly back towards the barn. The snow crunched under her feet and completely covered the top of her head, weighing her hair down and making some water run down into her eyes as it melted. Her house was literally a castle, while perhaps not as grand as the one she had been to in France, Chateau Chenonceau. When she had seen a castle for sale in Newfoundland she had just had to have it. It was a red and white brick building with three stories and a great view of the ocean. It had all the modern conveniences but was still made to look old-fashioned and decadent. She snorted a little, old-fashioned, she thought, *I certainly am part of the modern world. It is much more accurate to say that it looks like a place more familiar to me than most places I have lived in during this past century.* Staying in the tiny dorm had been only to help Joseph accept her in the beginning as a regular student. While she had been one, she was certainly not ordinary in any way.

The castle was jammed into the right side of a small hill and had a lovey view of the ocean. The barn had been her idea and had been built just a few weeks ago. It was all wood and was nestled in some trees just off to the side of Castle Mandeville, as she had been calling the place. She hoped that when Joseph was well and this was all over they could go to France. Her last trip there had been nothing but pleasant; meeting with the countess and having to bring her three women as victims. Yes, she hadn't been to Chateau Chenonceau in many years. It was so beautiful, all white with grey roofs, a drawbridge, and of course its unusual structure as it was built on a bridge itself over the river. She could hear the horses neighing and stomping their feet. Animals were usually leery of vampires and the poor creatures had every reason to be tonight. The smell of blood and the pounding of heartbeats must have awoken something in Joseph, as he stirred. "Blood." Cassandra was so happy to hear him speak.

"Yes, beloved, I know you need it and I know poor Jake will at least die for a reason." Joseph stood then and started to slowly make his way towards the barn. The horses inside made more noises and Cassandra decided to move in first and attempt to quiet them. She flung open the barn door and entered. Jake was a black mustang, with just a little white around his nose. He moved about in his stall and tried to break the rope tying him to the back where his water, oats, and hay were. She did as she had seen Joseph do many times; she extended her hands and used her telepathy. *Calm down, Jake, this is someone who is happy to meet you. You too, Eleanor, settle down, easy.* The calming thoughts seem to work and they both settled once more. The two mustangs had been quite expensive. Eeanor was all grey with a long mane and tail, and was ever so affectionate for a horse. Cassandra closed the stall door fully, and quickly put a handkerchief across the horse's brow to blind Eleanor. Cassandra hoped that if she didn't see what happened to Jake, it might make her suffer a little less.

Joseph lumbered in through the door. He was dragging the right side of his body and he was drooling. Cassandra had never seen him this way before and she hated it. He growled like an animal and his eyes glowed faintly red. Cassandra opened the stall door and wrapped both arms around Jake. He was no longer calm and he tried hard to buck and shake her off. Joseph seemed to quicken his pace and his legs gave out from underneath him. Cassandra tensed and almost went to help him but knew she could not, the horse was strong and it was all she could manage to hold him down. Joseph did not seem to notice any pain, and came forward on his hands and knees, soon latching onto the horse and pulling himself up. With Joseph's added weight, Cassandra let go for a second. She tied another rope around Jake's neck and fastened the other end to the stall door, making it very hard for the animal to move. Joseph dug in with his nails to the horse's side and his fangs went in. Jake violently objected and tried to shake him off, neighing loudly, but unable to free himself.

A tear slid down Cassandra's cheek, not so much for the horse, but for what Joseph had been reduced to. Eleanor was no longer quiet and she knew she had to get over there before she managed to break the rope tied to her harness. Cassandra knew that she too needed blood. At least a horse contained plenty of it. She knew that as long as she kept Joseph away, Eleanor would live through the night. Cassandra wiped away the tear and secured the horse as before, sending out calming thoughts, *this will hurt but you will recover. Focus on me and remain calm, nothing can be done for Jake now*. She glanced back and instantly regretted it, Jake had stopped protesting and she saw gushes of blood begin to stain the wall and floor. Whatever Joseph was now, he was certainly not the kind man she loved so dearly. Forced to let her own hunger take hold, she sunk her teeth into Eleanor's neck and let the blood run into her mouth and down her throat. The sounds that Joseph was making disgusted Cassandra; sucking and gulping noises mixed with the occasional squishing and cracking sound. The horse was dead, but in his feral state, Joseph must want every drop of blood. Cassandra drank just enough to feel full. She knew that Eleanor would be fine, and Cassandra bit her finger, and rubbed it over the puncture wounds to close them up.

She got out of the stall, wiped her mouth, and steeled herself for what would be a grisly sight. Joseph was drenched in blood as he left the stall. Something pink and rubbery fell from his lips, and in his hands were parts of the horse's ribs and intestines. She had seen gore, but this was on a whole different plateau. She retched for a second but soon regained her composure. Joseph seemed to smell the air and started to move toward Eleanor's stall. "No Joseph, you have savagely killed one horse and I won't let you do the same to her. You have plenty of blood for now, calm down." She kept her voice even and tried to stare him in the eyes. She reached out with her mind to his. *I know you must be somewhere in there, beloved. At least let me get you inside and clean you up.* Joseph's only response to was to first lick his lips, and then his fingers. Finally, he growled at her and advanced a few more steps toward the stall. She moved to get in front of him. His legs seemed to be working a lot better. She felt some small comfort that at least physically, the titanic amount of blood had seemed to help.

She saw the red in his eyes and watched his muscles tense. She moved and grabbed his shoulders. "Goddammit Joseph, I said no! That's enough!" She tried to reach his mind once more. *Stop this now, don't make me hurt you!* Once more his only response was a guttural growl and a fierce shove against her. She braced herself and he only made her budge a tiny bit. His strength was far from returning, and hers was near full once more. He seemed to become frustrated, and tried to head-butt her. She was done being gentle. She slammed her elbow into his left side and he staggered back. He lunged at her and tried to bite her with his fangs. Cassandra knew that she would have to end this quickly or one of them could be even more hurt. She darted to the side and rolled, seeing the metal saddle rack just off to the right. She knocked the saddle off and jumped forward. Joseph had already closed the distance and was about to break down the door to Eleanor's stall. The horse bucked and kicked, splintering the side panel and making a terrible neighing sound. Despite the blindfold, the horse knew instinctively that something was very wrong. Cassandra slammed Joseph in the gut with the metal handles of the rack, causing him to vomit blood. It drenched her shoes, but she ignored it. Bringing the bent rack upward with both hands, she caught him on the chin with a knockout blow. Joseph's eyes rolled up into his head and he collapsed to the floor. Fortunately the discarded saddle stopped his head from striking the hard concrete. Cassandra tossed the ruined stand aside and quickly retrieved the rope strapping on the wall that was used for leading the horses out of the barn. She tied his hands together and put him over her shoulder once more. Tears spilled from her eyes and her mind raced. *How long will he be in this condition? Did I just re-injure his poor brain that is trying to heal? How am I going to keep getting a supply of blood to him? What if his parents call, or one of his friends come looking for him?* She pushed those concerns aside. She had to deal with Joseph as he was right then until she had a way to secure him.

She entered through the door on the right side, directly beside the garage door, and went into the basement. Joseph was still unconscious and he was dead weight. Even with vampire strength, it was hard. She went past the new Chevy Volt, the Harley Davidson roadster, and the Cadillac ELR Convertible. She had not even had a chance to ride the bike or drive the convertible yet. She went to the right corner of the room to the grandfather clock. It looked old and seemed as if it no longer worked, but it held a purpose. She opened the glass and adjusted the time to 3:55, approximately the time she had seen Joseph as a boy and had left him her cat. The clock slid to the right, revealing a short staircase down. Cassandra had done so many fun things in this house for Joseph, she wondered if he would ever get to enjoy any of them. The clock went back into place as she entered the game room. She knew that Joseph liked a little bondage and she thought that sometime they might explore the idea more fully. In here was bondage gear, a bed, chains, and for now the most important part—sturdy restraints. Cassandra had had them reinforced with titanium, and knew that not even a vampire could break free from them.

It sounded like Joseph was stirring as he lay on the cast iron cushioned black metal table. Perhaps he had been just clearing his throat, but she couldn't take a chance. She didn't want to fight with him more and possibly get further hurt herself. Securing his arms and legs to the table, she took a moment to look at his head. Thankfully, their struggle in the barn had only caused bruising and little blood around his mouth, probably from his fangs biting into his lower lip. She examined his head wound and saw that while the brain was no longer visible, there was only the thinnest layer of bone over it and it was certainly very delicate. She was a medical doctor and couldn't help but be a little curious to see how his body would recover from such a grievous wound. She quickly applied the chin strap to hold his head in place, not knowing how much flailing about he might do in this state. His eyes snapped open and he lunged at her fingers. She was fast, but he managed to nick her hand and draw blood. Frustrated and angry, she lashed out with her other hand, slapping him hard across the jaw and causing a tooth to fly out. She instantly felt bad for doing it but knew it was purely instinctual. Putting her finger to her mouth, she tasted her own blood and held it there until it healed. Once more, a tear trolled down her cheek,

"My poor Joseph, I know you don't mean to hurt me. You act now out of pure instinct. You are more animal than man in your behaviour and you certainly aren't to blame. I'll sleep here in the room with you tonight, and tomorrow I'll seek out Mark. Assuming he's still in the province. He filled in for you before, and he can do so again." *I've fixed every problem before, and I can once again*, she thought.

"Arr! Blood. Grarr!" Joseph was angry and and was lashing out, trying to break his bonds. Cassandra tore up tiny pieces of a silk cloth and stuffed them in her ears. This was going to be a long night, and only the first of many. She thought to him, *Rest, beloved. You can't break free. One day you'll be whole again, and I'll be there with you.*

Section D:

Tales from other Authors

Author's Note

This section contains stories (and a poem) from other writers. I am a part of a group called Four Phoenixes Publishing. We are a group of authors that produce great writing, promote each other, and help each other out. I hope you'll check out our Facebook page. In the meantime, here's sampling of their work, along with author bios for each, enjoy!

Author Bio: Kevin Wright

Kevin Wright just can't stop sharing his quirkiness with the rest of the world—his offices are littered with overstuffed bookshelves, antique maps, and collections of weapons on the walls. Born and raised in Illinois, and a lifelong Chicagophile, he spent years teaching college-level courses in Logic and Critical Thinking, History, Communication, and Argumentation (even coaching the intercollegiate debate teams at Illinois State University), until he finally started putting his eclectic stories down on paper. His debut horror novel, *The Knight of Cups*, has garnered praise from reviewers, such as "There were times that I couldn't put it down because I just *had* to see what was going to happen to the characters," and "It is several genres that aren't usually combined, rolled into a cohesive and compelling tale. Somehow it manages to be suspenseful and hilarious at the same time." *The Knight of Cups* is available in both paperback and Kindle formats. For more information about Kevin, please go to his website at:

https://www.kevinwrightbooks.com

WAITING
by Kevin Wright

Waiting.
Sunlight.
Waiting.
Dusk.
Waiting.
Moonlight.
Hunting.
Hunting.
Finding.
Watching.
Smiling.
Watching.
Laughing.
Watching.
Growling.
Smelling.
Fear.
Running.
Chasing.
Fear.
Chasing.
Screaming.
Chasing.

Door.
Locked.
Growling.
Waiting.
Hiding.
Waiting.
Waiting.
Waiting.
Waiting.
Unlocked.
Door.
Pouncing.
Tearing.
Screaming.
Ripping.
Blood.
Feasting.
Laughing.
Waiting...

Author Bio: Joe Chianakas

Joe Chianakas is the author of *Rabbit in Red*, a horror trilogy. *Rabbit in Red* earned best horror book in the Summer Indie Book Awards. The first two books in the series were chosen by Horror Block to be sent to thousands around the world. You can find *Rabbit in Red* on most of your favourite book platforms. Learn more by visiting:

www.FrightFest4D.com

Or visit Joe's website at:

http://www.joechianakas.com

The Destroyer
by Joe Chianakas

Addie and I sat in my car late one warm winter night, two of last people on Earth who still wanted to enjoy the dirty taste of a cigarette. We were not-so-secret smokers. We tried to keep the house smelling clean, but in my 1999 piece of shit Chevy Cavalier, we didn't give a damn. Let the thing smell like an ashtray. It looked like one.

Normally, we'd have the heater on and the windows just cracked, but it was warm, especially warm for Missouri, considering it was the first of February.

"Climate change, they say," Addie told me as she took a long drag, the cherry tip of the cigarette burning bright. "Do you believe that?" She looked at me, her eyes weary from a long day of work. We'd finish these smokes then go to bed and start another same-o same-o work day in the morning. Addie was a middle school teacher. She was in her mid-twenties and had been teaching for a few years now, but she never smoked at work or in front of the kids.

I nodded. "At least we're not running the car tonight. Wasting gas and all." I took a long drag and coughed hard exactly at the same time I saw the truck down the road.

"Look at that." Addie pointed at the truck.

"What's that on the front of it?" I asked. As it approached, I could see that it was a huge semi, and it had some kind of funny face across the front grill. It was an emoji, the hysterical one, the laugh with tears rolling down its cheeks.

"Wonder what he finds so funny," Addie whispered.

I shook my head but didn't speak out loud. We were parked at the end of a cul-de-sak. We'd been renting a home here for a couple years now, and neither of us had ever seen the likes of a truck like that on our small town street. It nearly consumed both sides of the road.

"Maybe you should park in the drive way," Addie suggested.

I nodded but didn't move. The truck approached, and I felt frozen. There were only a few more houses behind me, and I wondered where the truck was going. We must have been the third house from the end of the block.

The truck crept closer.

And closer.

It approached the front of my shitty Chevy. The hysterical emoji looked so out of place, and for a second, realistic or not, I thought the truck might eat us. Like, literally, the mouth of the emoji would just open up wide and swallow the car with me and Addie in it.

"Jim, this is scaring me. Let's get inside the house."

I held up my right hand and said, "One minute. I want to see what he's doing."

The truck really did consume the road, but it didn't eat my car. It's right side rolled onto the sidewalk on the street across from us a bit, and it slid by us with maybe just a foot in between my car and the truck. I squinted and pressed my face against my window to try and see the driver's face. Just as the driver passed, a sliver of moonlight reflected over the driver's side window. But the truck's window was tinted, and I didn't see a face. That's when Addie opened her door.

"No!" I snapped. I don't know why I snapped at her, but something inside me said that it wasn't safe to go outside. "Wait."

The truck was no longer just on the sidewalk. It rolled up onto the front yard of the house across the street from ours. And then it stopped.

"Jim, I think we should call the police."

I reached into my pocket for my cell phone. As I brought it up in front of me, the truck's engine roared a barbaric yelp. I dropped my phone, and it slid right underneath the seat.

"Fuck." I sighed and reached for it. My hand hit some metal bar. They make it so easy for shit to slide underneath your seat, but impossible for anyone to retrieve it, I thought. "Addie, I can't get it. Can you try?"

She bent over, her head in between my legs and reached under my seat. In any other situation, I would have made a dirty joke, but tonight was far from the ordinary.

"Oh my God," I mumbled.

"Ouch!" Addie cried as she jerked up and hit her head on the steering wheel. "What is it?"

"Look!" I pointed at the truck. Its engine shouted again.

The truck lunged forward at an impossible speed. Nothing that big can have that kind of acceleration, right? I don't even know why I was thinking of that question. Shock can do strange things to the mind.

Having parked and roared its engine a couple of times in the front yard of our neighbor's home, the truck sped through the next neighbor's front yard to the last house on the right. But when it approached that house, it didn't stay in the front yard. It turned and drove right through the house.

Not just into it. Through it. The house, a ranch style single-family home, collapsed completely as if a tornado had just hit. It took nothing but a second.

Was the family home? Sure they were. It's late. They were probably getting ready for bed, and then BOOM!

Gone, in an instant.

I shook my head. How is this happening? And what the fuck am I am going to do?

"Addie, the phone, now." I reached out my hand to her, but I couldn't turn my eyes away from the destruction I had just witnessed.

"I couldn't get it," she said.

"Then give me yours."

"It's inside the house."

I looked at her then, then I looked at our house, and then back at the semi. It was backing up now, slowly.

Once again, I found myself frozen as I watched the truck back up onto the street. I considered my options. I could run in our house. Jesus, our puppy, our two cats! Could I just leave them there? What if the truck attacked our house?

Then I looked at the keys I had in the ignition. The car wasn't running, but I had turned the radio on so we could listen to some music while we smoked. I considered just getting the hell out of there.

The semi's engine growled again, a vicious and sickening noise. Then it charged forward once again. Before I could even blink, the truck had smashed into another house, the second one from the right at the end of the street. This house blew up, boards, debris, glass going everywhere.

"Jim, what the fuck are you doing?" Addie shook me. "We have to get the hell out of here!"

I started the car and we did exactly that.

I raced to the end of the street, and I was breathing hard, as if I had been sprinting instead of driving. Then behind me, I saw that damn emoji approach. It was faster than me, and in seconds, the damn laughing and crying face was inches behind.

It's going to eat us, I thought again.

"Oh, Jim, what are we gonna do?" I saw Addie's hands shoot up and cover her face. Then I heard the cries. Her cries had always been kind of awkward. She had cries that sounded like cute sneezes. There was always a girl you went to school with or worked with who sounded like a little bird whistling when she sneezed. That's how Addie sounded when she cried.

Despite everything, despite a monster truck that had crushed and destroyed two houses and was now chasing us, despite Addie, my girlfriend, the woman I had told myself I would eventually marry, despite it all, I smiled.

Then the truck hit my shitty Chevy from behind.

The seatbelt pulled tight against my chest, and Addie moaned.

"You okay?" I transformed into the soccer mom with my right arm fully extended across her body.

She turned her head slowly toward me, the way I'd picture a lizard turning its head just before eating its prey.

"No, I'm not fucking okay, Jim!" She pivoted in her seat and looked behind us. The beast of a truck had slowed. "What the fuck is he doing?"

I looked in the rear view mirror and saw what Addie had seen. The truck was turning around.

"It could have destroyed us, if it wanted. I don't know what it wants, but maybe—"

I froze. I don't know how I knew what I knew, but somehow I sensed an absolutely forbidding premonition. "It's going to our house. He's gonna destroy our house. And he wants us to see." I slammed on the breaks, thrust the car into reverse, and accelerated towards the demon.

"What are you gonna do?" Addie looked pale, a ghost under the moonlight.

"I have to stop him. Oh, Jesus, Addie, our babies."

Addie screeched and another awkward cry leaked out of her mouth. "Oh, Jim, you have to save them!" To others, they may have only been one little puppy and two cats, but to us, they were our fur-babies, and I had to get to them. I can't believe I even left them, I thought. But I didn't have any choice, did I?

The truck was much faster than my shitty Chevy, but I caught up to it before it destroyed anything else. It seemed to be waiting for me. It had once again turned itself around, and it faced me as I approached. The hysterically laughing emoji on the front of its grill mocked me. Parked at the end of the cul-de-sak, with two houses at the end already destroyed, the truck simply laughed at me.

Where are the neighbors? Where are the police? Somebody should be doing something!

Addie reached over to me. "What are you gonna do?"

I turned and faced her. "Okay. I'm gonna run in the house and scoop up the kids. You hop in the driver's seat. If he comes at you, drive away. Just swerve, and you can avoid him. If he comes at the house, honk. Don't let up, just honk, and I'll know." My heart was racing, and I felt myself breathing hard even though I had only been sitting. Addie reached for a cigarette and lit up.

"I don't know, Jim. We shouldn't ...why is this happening?"

"Why does anything happen, Addie?" She puffed on her Marlboro, and I exited the car.

I swear the emoji was animated or something. The grin looked wider. Such a sinister grin.

The first couple of steps I took were slow, and I kept my eye contact on the destroyer. Then I sprinted. I felt like I was back in school, running on the playground from the person selected as "It" as if my life depended on it. This time, though, it did.

I got into the house, and then I let myself look back. Nothing. The truck stood still. Snapping my head to Addie, I saw the glowing cherry of her cigarette.

"Chunk, Mikey, Mouth, where are you? C'mon guys!" Mikey ran to me right away. A tiny Dachshund, I was greeted by kisses and scooped him up. "Chunk, Mouth, where are you?" Cats were much more fickle creatures, and I worried they'd be harder to find. Time to bring out their kryptonite. I went into the kitchen and grabbed a pack of a hot dogs from the fridge. I opened the bag and waved it around the house. "Chunk? Mouth? Come here!" It worked almost instantly. One grey cat—Mouth—and my large orange cat who lived up to his name—Chunk—rubbed on my legs. Good, okay, now what? Shit, how am I gonna get all three out there?

That's when I heard the horn. My car's horn matched the power of the shitty Chevy. It sounded more like a dying siren, but nonetheless I knew it was time to get the fuck out. That semi had destroyed two houses in the blink of an eye. I looked behind and then I saw what I could use—a box! It wasn't very big. I had used it to carry in some wood for the fireplace, but it would suffice. I tossed the hot dogs into the box. Chunk jumped right in, but Mouth—always the more cautious of the two—looked up at me as if questioning my actions. "C'mon, Mouth." I moved Mikey to my left arm, grabbed Mouth with my right, and put him in the box. Then—and they were going to hate this but they'd have to make due—I put Mikey in with them. The cats hissed, but I grabbed the box before they could jump out. I picked it up, ran to the back door, and not one second too late either. As I stepped out back, the house exploded.

My home. Poof! Like that, it was gone.

I felt a pain in my chest and a gag in my throat. I swallowed back some vomit and ran.

Every fiber in every piece of wood blew up. I ran around the left side of the house. I could barely see—it was like a huge smoke bomb, a storm cloud of debris. Addie had turned around, and when she saw me, I could see her cry. She reached across the front and threw the passenger door open. I tossed in the box of our fur-babies, probably the only babies we'd ever have. Then I hopped in the back seat. Addie floored it, and I looked behind me.

The truck had backed up after destroying our home.

It faced us.

It flashed its lights. Somehow this made the truck look as if it was winking at me.

The emoji grinned and cried in laughter. The truck backed up slowly, and before we were out of its sight, I saw the driver roll down the window.

Could it be? No, it couldn't be him.

The driver looked like my father. But my father had died many years ago.

The driver winked at me, just like the headlights on the semi. Then he rolled up the window. The last thing I saw as we turned off our street was the beast of a truck accelerate toward another house.

I turned around and shook with a feeling of absolute coldness.

Addie looked at me in the rear view mirror. "Are you okay?"

Without looking at her, I said, "No. Most definitely not."

She nodded, understanding and not understanding all at the same time.

"Where should we go?"

Out of town? To hell? Anywhere but here? I thought of lots of things, but the answer that came out my mouth surprised me. "To my . . ." Am I really suggesting this? I pictured the man who stepped out of the semi. "We have to go to my father's grave."

"What?" Her eyes narrowed in the mirror. "Why?"

"Just go."

"But why?" She looked at me as if my suggestion was the most shocking thing of the night. Then she continued. "I thought ...didn't you tell me that your father tried to kill you once? That he was a bad man?"

I nodded. "Yes."

She shook her head. "First, we gotta go to the police."

"No. The graveyard. I'm serious, Addie."

I had never seen that expression on her face before. It was fear and confusion—but not at a demon truck destroying homes. It was fear and confusion directed at me.

"Just go."

"To the graveyard." She sighed. Mikey jumped on her lap and licked her face.

I shivered again. Addie didn't know it, but I knew something. Just like I knew the truck would return to destroy our house, I knew this story wasn't over. Not yet. In fact, I knew the real story would start at my father's grave.

Stories often begin with someone else's ending, don't they? I smiled and thought of that night, that night from many years ago.

I had no logical thoughts, really. Addie was probably right. We should have called the police. We should have tried to warn the neighbors. That truck—it was backing up and destroying homes one at a time.

And why?

I laughed. If that really was my father, it makes sense. When he was alive, he didn't just want to destroy my life. He wanted to destroy everyone's life around me, too.

So we raced to the grave. I needed to see it.

I needed to see that very hole where I had buried my father the day after I had murdered him.

☐

Author Bio: Jennifer L. Gadd

Jennifer L. Gadd is a life-long reader and writer who holds a deep interest in writing books that children and young adults will want to read with joy. She writes mostly fantasy and science fiction, as well as hi-lo books for struggling readers. Her novel *Cat Moon*, is the first in her young adult paranormal series, *The Were-Children*. *Finn and the Boys* is a picture book for very young beginning readers. Her most recent novel, *The Second Battle*, retells a story from Irish mythology for young adult readers. You can find out more about Jennifer's writing on her site at:

http://jennifergadd.wixsite.com/jenniferlgadd.

Samildánach: A Lughnasadh Story
by Jennifer L. Gadd

The young man dropped his pack on the sand with a thud and looked out over the sea. He longed to go back home, but he knew the place he'd left couldn't be his home any longer. The words Tailtiu, his foster-mother, had said to him echoed in his ears. She hadn't wanted to tell him, but he had charmed it out her easily enough. "It was prophesied before you were born that you are destined to kill your grandfather, King Balor, of the Fomori." Tailtiu had wept when she told him.

Lugh didn't remember any of the original circumstances of the story. All he remembered of his grandfather was a time when he was about three, and the old king had placed an apple on the ground out of his reach. Lugh had not toddled over to retrieve the treat. He had stretched out his hands towards it and willed it to come to him. He remembered Balor's astonishment at this feat, and how the old man had laughed with approval. He had seemed nice enough to Lugh.

Of his mother, he remembered nothing at all.

He picked up his bundle and trudged back away from the shoreline to find a place to make camp. His stomach growled. He desperately wanted supper to be his first order of business, but there was the horse to tend to do. Enbarr nickered softly and tossed his extravagant mane. What a gift Manannán had given him in Enbarr! With such a mount under him, he clearly looked like a young man of means. No one would think little of him or deny him hospitality. His brow furrowed with uncertainty.

Once the horse was tended to, Lugh turned his mind to his own supper. He cut a strip of leather and fashioned it to the end of his staff to make a sling. Finding a rabbit in the woods above the shore proved short work with such a weapon, and soon he had his fire built and his supper cooked.

Before he lay down to sleep, he wrapped himself in the cloak Manannán had given him as he'd left. It changed with all the colors of the sea and protected its wearer from any physical wound. It could not, however, protect Lugh from his own dreams and fears.

And that night he dreamed.

He was drowning, falling from a great height into the ocean, hitting the foamy surface and being sucked down into the briny waters. He struggled against the pull of the waves and the currents, the salt burning his eyes and lungs. Then, a deep voice murmured in his ear, "Quit fighting, boy! I've got you." Arms held him like bands around his waist. He leaned back against something hard and strong, and his rescuer carried him, swimming with firm, strong strokes.

He collapsed on the shore, coughing, and the quiet rumble spoke again. "Go on, get it all up, then. That's the best thing."

When Lugh had vomited up the last of the salty water, he pulled himself up to his knees and looked up at his rescuer. Manannán mac Lir sat back on his haunches watching him. Lugh started to stammer his thanks, but the older man only said, "Let's go home, lad."

Then the dreamed shifted, and he was standing before a large door demanding entrance. The man at the door was laughing at him, and Lugh could feel the anger boiling inside him.

"I am a warrior!" he insisted.

The doorkeeper laughed again. "A boy your age? Of course, you are."

"I am a musician! Let me play for you!"

"Oho!" was the answer. "A warrior and a musician. Fancy that."

Lugh burned with embarrassment. Who was this man to speak to him this way?

"I am Lugh, son of Balor, King of the Fomori! I demand entrance!"

"Indeed," fluted the doorkeeper in a sing-song voice. "And I'm the Queen of the Faeries!" He could hear the guffaws through the door.

Lugh's lip trembled despite his best intention, and a thin whimper escaped his throat. "Please," he begged, "let me be your cupbearer. I'll even do that." But the laughter continued unabated.

Lugh woke in a sweat, and the morning sun glared in his eyes. He threw off his cloak and lay back to catch his breath. In his dream, he could never think of a clever enough comeback to gain him entrance. He hated that dream, hated feeling so incapable, so left out, so weak.

As for the rest of it, he didn't really remember his grandfather's having thrown him and his brothers into the sea to drown, but he had wheedled the story out of Tailtiu so many times, he could dream it. His grandfather hadn't been so nice after all. There had never been a trace of his brothers. Oh, some folks said they had turned into seals. That didn't seem likely, but Lugh knew that even stranger things had happened. Regardless, Manannán had saved him and fostered him.

Manannán, Master of the Seas, had taken Lugh in as his son. Manannán, with his taut features, hair the color of bull kelp pulled back in a strip of leather, and stern countenance, had taught so many things to his eager student. Each new skill mastered earned a Lugh a rare, wintry smile of approval, and the first task had been learning to swim. Lugh's cheeks still flushed pink with pleasure when he recalled the day Manannán had tossed him off the boat and made him swim to shore. He'd swum the distance easily, and he knew that Manannán was proud of him.

His foster father had also arranged for tutoring with specialists in every field: smithing, farming, weaponry, music, poetry and every other skill and art. He'd had the best schooling imaginable, and he really could do all those things. Now he was setting out to find his fortune and his destiny, as far away from Balor and the horrible prophecy as he could get. Manannán had been exasperated at the boy for his refusal to accept his fate, but Lugh was determined that he would not kill his own grandfather. He just wanted to find his father's people and belong somewhere. He was relieved, then, when Manannán seemed to give up the fight and decided to allow him to journey to Tara. The Tuatha Dé Danann were preparing for war, and Manannán was convinced they needed Lugh's help.

As he broke camp the next morning, Lugh remembered another of the man gifts Manannán had given him. It was a breastplate, magic-wrought such that no weapon could pierce it. It was a heavy piece of armor, and Lugh decided it to wear it that day. It wouldn't do to go into battle not having tested his equipment. He couldn't say why it seemed to be important at the time, but his instincts proved to be excellent.

It was about midday when he heard hoofbeats in the distance. He kept a wary stance, but continued his journey to Tara. The hoofbeats grew louder and soon a figure could be seen riding towards him. He tensed. He knew no one in this part of the country, so it couldn't be a friend. Again his instincts did not fail him. The approaching rider looked unkempt and rough. The fine steed he was riding had obviously been stolen. A brigand, then. Lugh prepared to fight.

The thief, though, was a coward and had no intention of fighting in hand-to-hand combat. As he drew near, he flung a spear. Lugh, not expecting such a cowardly act, did not have time to move, and the spear struck him square in the chest. Stunned, and cursing himself for a fool, he slid off Enbarr's back and onto the ground. Manannán's armor proved its worth, though, and he was not wounded.

As the robber dismounted to claim his quarry, Lugh seized the spear and gutted the man through. "Vermin," Lugh muttered.

Lugh wiped off the spear and examined it. Crude, but efficient. He would keep it as the spoils of war, he thought. Someday, though, he vowed he would have a better weapon. He slapped the thief's horse on the backside and bid it go home to its owner.

As he turned to remount Enbarr, Lugh heard a low growl. He swung back around in time to see that the would-be robber had not been traveling alone. He had left behind a hound, who was now eyeing him with suspicion. He looked underfed and skittish. Lugh drew the last of the rabbit he had caught the night before from his pack and threw it to the dog, who caught it in midair. Lugh watched as the hound tore at the meat with frantic precision, as if he were afraid it would disappear before he could finish it.

"Poor thing," thought Lugh. He crouched low to the ground as the dog finished his meal, encouraging him in soft tones. The dog crept towards Lugh, timid and frightened, but when Lugh reached out to stroke his matted fur, the dog quivered with joy. "Good dog," said Lugh. "There's nothing wrong with you that a little care and training won't set right." The hound was not a great hunter and seemed not to have any special skills, but he was good enough for now. Lugh named the dog Failinis, because all of Ireland was his home.

Thinking back over the attack, Lugh knew he had been more lucky than skillful, and he vowed not to be caught off guard like that again. He was nothing if not a fast learner. He continued on his journey richer by a spear, a traveling companion, and a bit more wisdom.

The next day, Lugh approached the great hall of Tara, where Nuada of the Silver Arm held court. Flags were flying from the ramparts, which meant that the Tuatha Dé Danann were gathered there for a feast day. Lugh's mouth went dry. He stood before the door of the great hall, and he knew his worst nightmare had come true.

It was the door from his dream. He swallowed thickly, knowing what would come. He was glad he had worn Manannán's helm with its flashing stones to give him confidence. He felt at his side for reassurance and felt Manannán's sword, the Answerer, the wounds from which no man could recover. His foster father had provided for him well for this day. Failinis gave his hand a tentative lick, and Lugh smiled. And then he knocked.

The doorman opened the door and looked at him inquiringly.

"I am Lugh, the son of Cían, son of Dian Cécht and of Ethne, daughter of Balor. I wish to enter."

The doorman peered at the handsome young man. "No one enters Tara without practicing an art. What do you offer?"

"Ask me anything," replied Lugh. "I am a master builder."

The doorkeeper frowned. "We do not need that skill. Luchta provides it."

Lugh thought quickly. "Well then, I am a smith," he countered.

The doorkeeper's head shook. "We have a highly skilled smith in Colum. We don't need another."

Lugh felt the sweat pooling up under his arms and trickling down his neck. His dream was coming true, and they weren't going to let him in. They didn't want him. He listed all his skills—harper, warrior, poet, historian, brazier.

"Ask me anything. I am a physician!" Lugh said through clenched teeth.

The doorkeeper only shrugged and looked unimpressed. "We have Dian Cécht. Surely you agree he is the best physician in the land."

Lugh sucked in his breath. Dian Cécht was his grandfather, and he was inside. He had to get in. He sighed, "I will be your cup-bearer, if you'll have me."

All he got in return was a wistful smile. He should have known better than to think the court of Nuada would have no cupbearers. He turned away, resigned. Then he stopped. He had an idea.

He charged back at the doorkeeper and demanded, "Go ask your king if he has anyone in his service who can do all of those things!"

An eyebrow shot up, and the doorkeeper withdrew. A moment later, he returned. "The king wishes to speak with you," he said.

He had done it! He had finally gotten past the door. They wanted him after all!

But when Lugh entered the great hall of Nuada, his stomach sank. The room was filled with stony faces, murmuring to one another. He could hear snatches of conversation.

"Another foundling of Manannán, isn't he?" said Aengus mac Og.

Sitting next to him was an older man Lugh did not recognize, who smirked back at Aengus. "Can't have been tested, can he? Arrogant little popinjay."

Lugh gulped as the king spoke to him. "So you are the Samildánach, the Many-Skilled One, are you? Lugh heard more than one person the crowd snort with laughter. "You understand we will require proof?" Lugh nodded.

Nuada rapped on the table. "And where is my champion?" Lugh watched with some relief as the older man stood up and acknowledged the king.

"Ogma," Nuada said, "by all rights, you have the testing of the boy."

"This," thought Lugh, "shouldn't be too difficult. He's old. I can beat him in combat." Lugh watched as Ogma stretched out his arms and shoulders, as if shaking off the lethargy of the feast. To his great surprise, the older man reached down and with a growl that filled the hall, tore one of the huge flagstones out of the floor of the hall, and hurled it through the wall, where it landed outside in the courtyard. He didn't even break a sweat.

Lugh looked back at where Ogma had been sitting. There was a war club hewn from a blackthorn tree propped against the wall. Lugh certainly hoped he was never on the wrong end of it.

He licked his lips. He could do this. He knew he could. He hoped he could.

So he stepped through the hole in the wall. He took a deep breath. Then he picked up the flagstone and threw back into the hall, where it landed on the floor exactly as it had been. He then picked up the piece of the stone wall, and with muscles straining and sweat pouring off his back, he thrust it back into the wall. When he returned to the hall before all those assembled, it was absolutely silent.

Lugh stared at the place where the hole in the wall had been just minutes before. Had he really done that? He looked down at his scratched hands in surprise, and then up quickly to the staring crowd. Ogma man caught his eye, and he moved quickly to make his face implacable, to look as if he had planned it all along.

But he was a fraction of a second too late. The older man knew. Would he betray him before all his father's people? Tell them he hadn't known for certain he could do it? Then Ogma gave him a lop-sided grin.

"Well done, lad," he said, his eyebrows still raised in surprise at having been bested by one so young. "Well done." With that, he gave Lugh a congratulatory slap on the back that nearly sent him sprawling.

Ogma gestured to a servant and said, "Bring the boy something to eat and drink. I tell you he's earned it this day!" When Lugh was settled with a full plate and cup, Ogma placed a harp at the young man's feet. "After you've finished," he laughed, "you can sing for your supper."

Acknowledgements

First off I want to thank my wife, Joanne, for always being there for me. I'm a lucky man to have her, as she always gives me good advice, is willing to help in her own way with any plan I have, and is my constant companion. I could not do this without her love and support. My friend said she has the patience of Job. I'm not a religious guy, and I'll admit that sometimes I can be hard to live with. I'm glad I found someone who is able to stick by me through thick and thin.

I want to thank all of the fans, both recent and those that have been there since the beginning, for purchasing this short story collection. I've loved short stories my whole life and have been writing them since I was ten years old. I just felt that most of what I wrote back then (and really up until a few years ago), wasn't worth publishing. Recently I've listened to a lot of short stories, read a bunch, and even had the pleasure of getting one published a few years ago that you'll find that here. I decided that it was time for a little break from my *Newfoundland Vampire* series, but have no fear, book four is already half done and I've included the first two chapters of it here. I'm still self-published with some other wonderful authors on a team, and as I'm enjoying all the freedom, I'm going to stick with it for at least a little while longer. That said, I'd like to promote my group, Four Phoenixes

Publishing, and I hope that when you're done with this book you'll consider reading other great novels by Jennifer L. Gadd, Joe Chianakas, and Kevin Wright.

I want to thank my new editor, Heather Reilly. Heather is a pleasure to work with. She has made editing this collection as painless as possible, has given me lots of great feedback and made my stories even better. She has helped me on my journey of always growing as a writer and I want to thank her for that. Her notes are both helpful and insightful.

My friend John has always been a great sounding board, which is greatly appreciated.

My parents have never stopped believing in me and encouraging my writing.

Kevin Kendall has done some amazing artwork, and I feel privileged to have it grace the cover of these pages. He was very accommodating to my very specific ideas and was a pleasure to deal with. He lives here in Newfoundland, and I encourage you to check him out at Kendallight Studios on the web.

I'm flattered that you've come to join me for my short stories, and I hope that you enjoy reading them as much as I delighted in writing them. I'm always happy to hear from anyone, so feel free to contact me through my website.

Until next time, I'll leave you with another line from one of my favorite songs. Listen to it, and while I don't encourage worry, I hope it will make you more aware of the fragile state that this world and all of the people in it are currently in.

"This is the world we live in, and these are the hands we're given. Use them and let's start trying, to make this a place worth living in." -Genesis, "Land of Confusion."

About the Author: Charles O'Keefe

Charles O'Keefe lives in the beautiful province of Newfoundland, Canada, with his wife and two feline 'children,' Jude and Eleanor. He is a part-owner of a beauty wholesale business. He enjoys many hobbies and activities that include reading, gaming, poker, Pilates, Dungeons and Dragons, and of course, fantasizing about vampires. Charles is the author of three books in the *Newfoundland Vampire* series, but this is his first collection of short-stories. Look for the fourth *Newfoundland Vampire* book sometime in the near future.

To find out more about Charles or his other books, go to Twitter and Facebook or visit his web site at:

http://www.charlesokeefe.com

Other books by Charles O'Keefe:

The Newfoundland Vampire Book I

The Newfoundland Vampire Book II: Killer on the Road

The Newfoundland Vampire Book III: The Gathering Dark

Upcoming Books:

The Newfoundland Vampire Book IV: War of the Fangs

Find out more about the author and his books on:

Twitter
Facebook
Goodreads

And on his website at:

http://www.charlesokeefe.com